THE
NORTH POLE
PROJECT

IN SEARCH OF THE TRUE MEANING OF CHRISTMAS

D. MICHAEL MACKINNON

Post Hill
PRESS

DEC   2017

A POST HILL PRESS BOOK
ISBN: 978-1-68261-532-4
ISBN (eBook): 978-168261-533-1

The North Pole Project:
In Search of the True Meaning of Christmas
© 2017 by D. Michael MacKinnon
All Rights Reserved

Cover art by Christian Bentulan

Post Hill Press
New York • Nashville
posthillpress.com

Published in the United States of America

For all those who still believe in Christmas.
This book and this special place is for you.
And most especially for my Leela June, who always believes in...me.

CHAPTER ONE

At the very depth of his depression and mentally lost beyond all reason, Christian Nicholas wandered from room to room to room in his thirty-thousand-square-foot mansion in a secluded section of Westwood, Massachusetts, wondering not only where it all went wrong, but if he could somehow find the inner strength needed to defeat the darkest thoughts now filling his broken mind.

As the very handsome, tanned, tall, and athletic fifty-four-year old Nicholas shuffled aimlessly from one of his twenty-eight rooms to the other, he kept coming back to his richly appointed dark-paneled home office. Each time he arrived back at the office, he would sit behind his massive, twenty-thousand-dollar desk and stare at a two-inch-tall plastic Nativity scene he had since he was a little boy. Next to it were two opened prescription bottles of sleeping pills and a twelve-ounce Waterford crystal glass filled with ice water.

Every time he sat, he would silently go through the same routine. He would run the fingers of his right hand through his thick, black-and-steel-grey hair, use the same hand to rub the three-day growth of beard on his face, and then lean back in the chair and rock back and forth as he stared more and more intently at the pills.

He would then stand and walk around his multimillion-dollar home all over again, arriving…as he had the three previous times, right back in his home office sitting and staring at the bottles before him.

But this time was different. This time, Nicholas did not stand up again to pace and to think. This time, he sat silently in the chair without moving. After several minutes of shifting his bloodshot eyes from the Nativity scene, to the bottles, to the water glass, and then finally back to the bottles again, he closed his unnaturally blue eyes and seemed to go into a trance.

As he sat there lost in cascading thoughts of depression and hopelessness, a lone tear escaped his closed left eye and made an irregular track down his tanned but haggard face.

The tear seemed to snap him out of his trance. Ever so slowly, he opened his eyes. And then, even slower, reached his left hand out until his fingertips lightly touched the faces of Joseph, Mary, and the Baby Jesus of his precious Nativity scene. Once done, he moved his hand slightly until it was next to one of the opened bottles of sleeping pills. Once there, he circled his fingers around the small, brownish plastic container and, inch by inch, brought it toward him.

CHAPTER TWO

Christina Marie ever so gingerly stepped off the city bus at the corner of Columbia Road and Hamilton Street in the Dorchester section of Boston.

It was 8:30 PM on a Friday night and she was beyond physically exhausted. Christina had just put in a ten-hour shift at the General Mail Facility in South Boston, her place of employment for the last eleven years.

Twelve years plus a couple of months before she stepped off that city bus, she had graduated with honors from Howard University in Washington, DC. But after one solid year of looking for a job in her chosen field with no success, she took her cousin up on his offer to put in a good word for her at the post office facility in South Boston where he worked.

He did and she got the job. As a "rookie" at the General Mail Facility, she immediately found herself working the overnight shift her first two years.

Christina was more than fine with the overnight shift and the long hours. She knew she was blessed even to have a job and she had hit her knees in prayer a number of times to thank God for her good fortune.

After putting in her time on that shift and learning the ropes, she was finally able to transfer to the 8 AM to 4 PM shift. A shift she loved and had worked joyfully for the last ten years.

But now…she no longer cared. While physically alive and whole, Christina Marie knew that her life as she knew it was over.

As the city bus made its way down Columbia Road toward Roxbury, Christina turned her head and looked at the triple-decker she lived in, half-way up the fairly steep hill that was Hamilton Street.

Even after all this time, just looking up at her home caused her brown eyes to fill with tears and streak her still beautiful face.

With great effort, she forced one foot in front of the other as she shuffled her way up in hill in the growing darkness.

Six months earlier, she had gone to her supervisor in the Post Office to request as much overtime as they could give her. Not because she needed the money, but because she did not want to go home. She could not stand the sounds of silence. A silence now broken only by her occasional sobs of inconsolable grief.

Three weeks before she requested all the overtime the Post Office could give her, Christina Marie had lost her only child to the streets. An innocent and beautiful twelve-year-old girl who found herself in the wrong place at the wrong time as she stumbled into street gang "justice."

While she was in college, Christina met "Mr. Right," married him without really thinking things through, and then endured the heartache of watching "Mr. Right" leave her for another woman on campus just a few months later.

But from that failed marriage had come the most amazing gift of all. A precious little baby girl who—with a large assist from her mom and her brother—Christina was able to nurture and raise on her own.

Christina became a single-mom who dedicated every waking second of her life to the welfare of her daughter. A daughter who had filled her life, her home, and her heart with pure joy.

Christina had always been a woman of tremendous faith. A person who not only could not wait to attend church on Sundays, but who was always anxious to put into action the wise words of her minister.

But when the streets took her daughter, Christina walked away from her church, from her faith…and from life.

CHAPTER THREE

Just as Christian slid the very expensive water glass toward him, he noticed the prism effect of his desk lamp shining through the fine Irish crystal. As he stared at the multiple colors shimmering off his finalized divorce papers resting on the corner of his desk, his iPhone began to ring.

He ignored the ring and let it go to voicemail. After the third time of someone calling nonstop, he fished into the pocket of his blue robe, answered the phone and screamed, "WHAT?" as loud as he could.

In response to his scream, he heard quiet laughter and instantly recognized the voice of his older brother Paul, who was now a minister down in Texas.

"I don't think mom would have approved of you screaming at me like that. Especially considering my calling in life."

Without taking his eyes off the vibrant colors being reflected onto the white paper and as he felt the energy draining from his mind and body, Christian answered his brother.

"Sorry, Paul. I don't think I can talk right now."

There were a few seconds of silence before his brother spoke.

"And that is precisely why you *have* to talk to me right now, little brother. After our conversation last night, I had a vision. A vision of you standing on the edge of a cliff. So, I'm begging you to talk to me right now and I'm begging you to back away from the bottomless pit you are now staring down into."

Christian let out a slight laugh. "But I'm not looking down into a pit. I'm in my office looking at my desk."

"Christian. You know *exactly* what I'm talking about. I need you to talk to me. I need you to tell me that you are not going to do anything stupid…or sinful. I need you to tell me that you are going to be okay until I can fly up there."

The multibillionaire who owned every single thing those who chase materialism could dream of, suddenly broke down and started to sob openly.

"Paul," he cried. "I'm so very tired. So very tired. I miss mom and dad so much. I just want to go to sleep and wake up in their arms like I did as a child. I miss mom and dad, and I want to go live with them now."

This time, it was the minister who screamed.

"No. No. You will *never* see mom and dad again if you take that step into darkness. Never. They want you to be happy. I know they do. But they want you to be happy here on earth for many more years before both you and I join them and Jesus in Heaven. Mom and dad believed in you, Christian. They loved you more than anyone. They were—and are—so very proud of you and all the gifts you have. Honor them, Christian. Honor them now with your gifts."

"How?" asked the billionaire as his tears dripped down onto his chest and onto his desk. "How?"

"By going back in time."

"What…what does that even *mean*?" Christian asked as his voice began to rise again.

"After we talked last night," Paul said in a voice of deep concern and fear. "I could not sleep one wink. I was up all night thinking about you and about what once made you happy."

Christian used the right sleeve of his by now gamey blue robe to wipe his eyes and running nose.

"And did you think of anything? Because for the literal life of me, I can't think of one thing now that makes me happy. Not one."

"That's the whole point," replied Paul with a glimmer of hope. "That's what I mean by going back in time. Nothing *now* makes you happy. Nothing. As soon as you got into high school you changed. You became so focused on a career with one of the big banks. You got into Harvard, and then you became even more focused on money. Then you struck it rich with your own hedge fund and married the "perfect" trophy wife to show off to your friends. Then your "perfect" life with your "perfect" wife fell apart in a big way. So what are you left with now, little brother? What? Billions of dollars, all the toys your hedonistic lifestyle demanded, and...*nothing*. Other than money, fame, and superficial looks, what do you believe in? Is there one shred of faith left in you? If there is—and I *know* there is—then call on it. Lean on it. In a world going more insane and faithless by the day, what does that shred of faith still left in you tell you? What can make you *happy* again?"

Nicholas lowered the phone next to his side as he tried once again to compose himself.

"Nothing...obviously," he finally replied.

"Nothing...*now*," his brother stressed again. "Nothing now. But sometime around 4 this morning, it hit me. Your mission in life hit me."

"And what might that be, my spiritual and holy brother," asked the billionaire as he put his phone on "Speaker" and reached again for the glass of water before him in quiet desperation.

"*Christmas*," his brother replied. "Christmas."

Just hearing the word froze Nicholas in his place. With one hand holding the bottle of pills and the other around the glass of water, he suddenly could not move as his brother's answer took him by complete surprise and shock.

"What about Christmas?" Nicholas was finally able to mumble.

"Don't you remember? When we were little kids and you were around six, seven, and eight years old, Christmas meant *everything* to you. The story of the birth of the *Baby Jesus* meant *everything* to you. It made you the happiest I have ever seen you. But you were happy not because you wanted presents, but because you wanted to honor Him by helping the other children on the Army bases we lived on who had lost a father to war or had it worse than us. Don't you remember? At six, seven, and eight years of age, you became a little Santa Claus for these children no older than you. You told mom, dad, and me that this was how you were '*Going to honor the Baby Jesus.*' With the money you made from collecting bottles and cans, you not only bought as many little presents as you could, but you wrapped each one yourself—and with your little plastic Baby Jesus Nativity scene faithfully and always in your pocket—you delivered each and every one by yourself. For years and years afterwards, Mom told me the pure love, faith, generosity, and giving you showed then made her the proudest of her entire life. Her *entire* life, Christian. Please…think about that. *Think* about what made mom so proud."

***

Still unable to move, Nicholas tried to force his mind to work through the haze of its pain, confusion, and deep depression to remember those very innocent and happy days. With his eyes now closed, he began to see flashes of those long-ago times. Flashes of his little *Baby Jesus*, flashes of little children smiling and crying in happiness. Flashes of *him* actually smiling in happiness.

Nicholas suddenly shook his head and turned his face toward the phone resting on his desk.

"I do remember, Paul. I do. But that was decades and a lifetime of misery ago. How does that help me…now?"

When his minister brother answered, it was the last thing he ever expected to hear. And the *only* thing that might save him.

"Become that person again, Christian. Honor Baby Jesus again. Recreate the good you did as a child but only now, on a massive scale. Lord knows you have the means. Let your faith guide you as you figure out how to become a Santa Claus all over again, Christian. Become Santa Claus. And in the process, heal and save yourself."

CHAPTER FOUR

Ten minutes after his brother Paul had hung up, Christian still had not moved. He had not moved one muscle other than to involuntarily blink.

His left hand was still wrapped around the bottle of pills with his right hand still holding the crystal glass full of water. The only difference now being that over the minutes, the warmth from his right hand had melted the ice in the glass. More than that, the condensation that had collected in little drops on the outside of the glass had rolled down the sides to form a small puddle at the base of the glass.

As Christian blinked, he finally shifted his eyes to look at the small but expanding puddle around his glass, which had now reached his little Nativity scene. And as he did that, his mind began to ever so slowly work again.

As it did, he tried to replay the conversation he had just had with his older brother over and over again in his mind. As he did that, seven words kept ringing out louder than all the rest:

"Become a Santa Claus all over again...Become a Santa Claus all over again...Become a Santa Claus all over again."

Even through his foggy and cloud-covered mind, Christian knew that his brother the minister was speaking in metaphorical terms. His brother was counseling—*begging* him, really—to literally save himself by finally putting the needs of others before himself for a change. To figure out a way to help others and in the process, maybe help himself.

***

Christian understood at least that much. But…he had never been much of a metaphorical person. Ever. He had always felt that one of the keys to his success, at least in business, was that he generally saw things *only* in black and white.

Christian knew that while he was blessed with a very good mind, he was most comfortable processing things in a literal way.

Knowing that, his mind reached out again for those seven words. "Become a Santa Claus all over again…Become a Santa Claus all over again."

As that phrase bounced around inside of his mind, he shifted his eyes from the bottom of the glass, to the bottle of pills folded into his left hand.

As he continued to process those words and the thoughts suddenly starting to form around them, he managed to move his head instead of just his eyes.

The unbathed-for-days multibillionaire turned his entire head to look from the pills to the water glass and then back at the pills. He then leaned forward and took a very hard and very long look at his little Nativity scene. Then, ever so slowly, he relaxed his grip on the pills, let go of the little plastic container, and brought his left hand back toward his chest. After a few deep breaths, he repeated the process with his right hand.

Once done, he began to repeat the phrase in his head over and over again. Soon, he was saying the words out loud. Except each time he repeated them out loud, he increased the volume of his voice until he was basically yelling.

"Become a Santa Claus all over again…Become a Santa Claus all over again."

Christian Nicholas then leapt out of his office chair with more energy than he had experienced in weeks. With every second, the newfound excitement and energy now flowing through him was not only clearing his mind, but vanquishing the darkness which had all but enveloped it.

"I wonder…" he said aloud as he brought both of his hands up to his head in amazement of the idea now crystalizing in his mind.

"I wonder…I wonder."

He then looked down at the phone on his desk and as he did, new tears began to fill his eyes and overflow onto his face. But for the first time since he could remember, they were tears of hope. Tears of pure joy.

"I'm not the genius in this family," Christian shouted while looking at the phone. "*You're* the genius, older brother. You're the genius and I'm going to make you...and mom and dad...proud. I am."

With that, he bent down and grabbed his little Nativity scene with his left hand and then, with his right, swept the two bottles of pills off the desk with such force that they peppered his office window like hail in a thunderstorm.

CHAPTER FIVE

For the first time in three days, Christian Nicholas was physically clean and much clearer of mind.

After showering, shaving, and brushing his teeth, he stepped into his closet to pick out some clothes to wear. When he did, he was hit with an instant and overriding wave of embarrassment and shame.

His "walk-in closet" was actually something more than eight-hundred square feet of ultra-luxurious storage space. Larger and more opulent, Nicholas knew, than the entire homes of many people living paycheck to paycheck in the United States and around the world.

"My closet," he thought as his mind was quickly, permanently, and continually shedding itself of the materialism and hedonism Nicholas had filled it with for the last few decades. "Says all that has been wrong with my values."

He then looked toward the ceiling.

"Please forgive me," he said out loud. "And give me the chance to make all of this right."

He then grabbed a pair of black khaki pants and a long-sleeve blue shirt and practically jumped out of the closet back into his bedroom.

As he was getting dressed, he began what would be eight phone calls in a row. The first was to his executive assistant Nina Sobhan, who was also a Senior Vice President in his company.

"Nina. Hey it's me. Yeah, I am back among the humans. I am heading down to our office on Main Street in about thirty minutes. I'm about to email you a list of the people I need to meet with when I get down there. If they can't get there, we will link them in via video conference."

His next call was to Ed Rogers. Rogers was the chairman of the most influential lobbying shop in Washington, DC. Democrats, Republicans, Independents, The White House, or Congress, Rogers could get to them all, one way or another. Nicholas knew Rogers and his team were the best, and it was for that reason he had placed them on a high five-figure-a-month (plus bonus) retainer for the last ten years.

"Ed," said Christian as he was putting on his right sock. "Yeah, I'm fine. Just a little bump in the road. Who cares what the media says. Look, I'm about to embark on the project of *my* lifetime and I am going to need all the help I can get in Washington…and then some. This is beyond confidential and during and after the process, it's going to have to stay off the books and remain off the books…*forever*. I'll tell you in person. Can you get away this afternoon? Great. I will have my jet pick you up on the way back from Boca Raton. What's in Boca Raton? The first and maybe most important piece of the puzzle. See you in a few hours."

By the time he was in the back seat of his chauffeur-driven Bentley, he was on his last call before reaching his rather nondescript four-story office building on Westwood's main street just opposite the town's middle school.

Christian Nicholas's personal wealth was just over $15 billion. His purposely mysterious hedge fund, which *The Wall Street Journal* once labeled "Darth Vader's Vault," managed well-over $200 billion in assets. One of those companies was a small, very private, and exceptionally inventive construction company the Pentagon and the three-letter agencies of the U.S. government quietly used to design and construct their most challenging, secure and secretive buildings. The good news was, they were headquartered the next town over in Norwood.

"Jeff, it's Christian. What? No," he stressed to his fellow CEO. "You know better than to believe anything you read or watch. Listen, can you get over to my office in about an hour? No, I can't tell you over the phone. Let's put it this way, we are both going to be under that *Get Smart* 'Cone of Silence' gadget when we talk. Yeah. See you then."

CHAPTER SIX

Joan Randall took a quick sip of coffee as she sat in the fifteen-by-twenty-foot English courtyard of her two-story townhouse in Boca Raton, Florida. As she put the cup back down on the glass outdoor tabletop, she let out a long, slow breath as she looked up at a portion of the bright blue sky showing between two palm trees.

This was the first business day in twenty-five years that the forty-six-year-old woman did not have to go to work. She did not have to go to work because she had announced her retirement as the president of Carnival Cruise Line a month earlier, and this past Friday had been her last day.

It wasn't that she didn't like working for Carnival; the truth was, she *loved* working there. She considered it the best company in the world and perfect for her workaholic, anal mindset.

And it was for that reason, she knew she finally *had* to quit.

Right after graduating college, she had become a reservations agent for Carnival and over the course of the next twenty years had worked her way up the corporate ladder until she was named president of the most popular cruise line in the world.

For the last five years, the five-foot seven-inch dark-eyed and dark-haired woman had put in sixty- to eighty-hour work weeks—often including weekends—to stay on top of a company designed to give average hard-working people a much-needed break from the demands of work and life. And *that*, knew Joan, was the ultimate irony.

While working overtime to make the lives and vacations of Carnival passengers as fun and fantastic as possible, she neglected to have a life of her own.

Twenty-one years of age soon became thirty. Thirty then turned to forty in the blink of an eye.

In the meantime, Joan Randall had become "beyond successful" by anyone's business definition of the words. She had been featured a number of times on CNBC, had been on the covers of *Fortune* and *Forbes*, had a great salary and perks, and because of her striking good looks and a figure maintained by early morning runs and daily home gym workouts, had also regularly attracted the attention of a number of male CEOs and even a few well-known media personalities.

But…other than the occasional date, her life and her time had been consumed by her career and *only* her career.

That was until Janice, her married sister and mother of two, had driven five hours down from Jacksonville just over a month ago to basically stage a one-woman intervention with her older and "famous" sister.

"You not only *need* to get a life," her younger sister had pleaded with her in the very same courtyard a few weeks earlier. "You *deserve* to have a life. A life that is about you. A life that feeds your soul, your faith, and your emotional needs. A life that is not defined by making one company shine…no matter how good it may be."

As Joan Randall sat in her shaded courtyard wearing royal blue workout pants, a white tee shirt, and a Miami Heat baseball cap wondering what that life described by her baby sister would look like, her phone rang on the table in front of her.

She slowly shifted her dark—almost black—eyes to look at the face of the smartphone. She had sworn to herself that no matter who called that morning, she was going to have the strength to ignore it.

She would have done so, except on the second ring, she noticed that instead of a number, her phone had spelled out "Unknown Caller" on its screen. Thinking it might be the CEO of the parent company of her former employer, she picked it up, swiped the face, and said, "Hello."

"Hi," said a deep male voice. "Is this Joan Randall?"

So…Joan thought. *Not* the CEO I had suspected.

"Yes, it is. Who is calling, please?"

The man cleared his throat and then paused a couple of seconds before answering.

"Hi, Joan...oh, I'm sorry. May I call you Joan?"

"Yes," said Joan with just a slight smile on her face. "If you tell me who *you* are."

"Yes. Right. Of course. My name is Christian Nicholas. You may not remember me, but we met a few years ago in a green room at CNBC. I was there to talk about hedge fund stuff and you were there to talk about actual real work."

Joan laughed out loud. She did indeed remember him. He was hard *not* to remember. Tall, tan, athletic, obviously very bright, looked like a movie star, but also...clearly full of himself, arrogant and if memory truly did serve, somewhat condescending.

"Yes, Mr. Nicholas. I do remember you."

"Please," said the deep voice. "Call me, Christian. So...I am calling out of the blue for two reasons really. The first, which is long overdue, is to apologize for the way I came across that day at CNBC. I think the technical definition for me that morning was that I was a '*jerk*.' I was actually incredibly impressed by you, and, like an immature jerk, shifted into full braggart, name-dropping and condescension mode..."

Joan suddenly felt her face go warm and as it was still a very pleasant seventy-four degrees in her shaded courtyard, she was fully aware that the Florida heat and sun were not to blame.

An unexpected reaction to say the least.

"...and I simply and sincerely wanted to apologize for that boorish and juvenile behavior. Even though it was only a few years ago, I have suddenly grown up quite a bit since then."

"Well," fibbed Joan as she took off her hat and fanned her face. "I don't really even remember you coming across that way, so no need to apologize."

"Please," said the deep and now calming voice. "I insist. Please accept my apology."

Joan laughed as she felt her face thankfully start to go back to its normal temperature.

"Fine...Christian. I accept your apology. Now, you said there was something else you wanted to discuss."

Just as he again cleared his throat to answer, Joan jumped back in. "...Wait a minute. Before you tell me, exactly *how* did you get my cell number?"

"How did I get...well...ah, I think...well...I'm not exactly sure how it was obtained, to tell you the truth. Only that one of my assistants emailed it to me this morning."

"I guess she's a good detective."

"He, actually," laughed Nicholas.

"Whoops," answered Joan. "Before I assume anything else, you were about to tell me the second reason for your call."

That was met by silence for a good ten seconds or so. Joan looked at the corner of the face of her phone to see if she had lost signal, but noticed she still had five bars. As she brought the phone back up to her left ear, she thought she could hear a hint of breathing.

"Christian. Mr. Nicholas. Are you still there?"

"Yes, sorry. I was just trying to organize my thoughts. Okay, so here goes. The good news for me is that I just had an epiphany of sorts. The bad news is that ever since it happened, my thoughts seem to be all over the place. With that said, I really *was* impressed by you when I met you that day at CNBC. To be honest, my first thought was 'the face of Audrey Hepburn and the figure of Raquel Welch.' Then you spoke and my next thought was, 'I'm *way* out of my league here.' Hence, the jerk in me came out trying to impress you with nonsense..."

There was another brief pause and Joan thought she heard the sound of someone drinking something.

"You know," she laughed before he went on. "You do have a 'Mute' button on your phone."

Christian laughed out loud and relaxed a bit more.

"Yeah, I know. But I need a 'Mute' button for my mouth more than for my phone."

They both laughed before he continued.

"Anyway...ever since that day, I tried to keep an eye on you and your career with Carnival."

Joan did not know how to respond to that and said as much.

"Christian, I'm not sure..."

"Joan, trust me. I'm not sure of anything at the moment other than to follow my instincts. One of them being to call you."

"Christian," answered Joan as she watched a bright red cardinal land on the gate of her back fence. "What *exactly* is it you want of me? Why are you calling?"

"Why? Because I am embarking on the most special project of my life—and I truly believe one of the most special projects of all time when it comes to helping poor children—and I was hoping you could sit down with me to talk about it in person."

Even though the call and her initial emotions caught her a bit off guard, Joan was still a highly accomplished, tough, though now *former* CEO, and quickly found her business footing.

"I see. And when would you like to meet?"

"This afternoon, if possible."

Joan laughed. "This afternoon? Are you serious? Where are you located?"

"I live up in Westwood, Massachusetts, and have a little office on Main Street in town."

"Massachusetts…this afternoon…how…"

"Joan. Wait. I looked on Google maps. There is an executive airport about one mile from your townhouse. One mile. If you say yes, I will have my jet pick you up there in about three hours. So…please say 'Yes.'"

Joan smiled to herself at the craziness of it all as she thought, this is not what her baby sister had in mind when she said she "needed to get a life."

CHAPTER SEVEN

Aside from Christian Nicholas, six other people sat around the long rectangular conference table built to seat twenty.

The conference room itself was simple, but still clearly luxurious, and designed for business efficiency. Dark paneled throughout with eighty-inch television screens at either end of the large windowless room and every state-of-the-art hi-tech device an executive could need was placed strategically throughout. The room was lit by stylish traditional lamps throwing off soft yellow light as Christian had always found them warmer and more comforting than overhead lights.

All of the six people present had signed an airtight nondisclosure agreements upon entering the office building. Those six were Nina Sobhan, Ed Rogers, Jeff Foster, Gerald Donovan (the Fund's general counsel), Marty Williams (a former Special Forces and Central Intelligence Operative who was now head of security), and Joan Randall.

Christian sat at the head of the table and slowly spun a Bic pen in circles as he fought a case of nerves he had not expected to have when he walked into the room.

He was not nervous at the thought of addressing the people now before him. Five of the six were either friends or long-time business acquaintances.

Those five didn't make him nervous in the least. It was the last person to walk into the room who now made him a little skittish.

***

As she stopped before him, re-introduced herself, and shook his hand with her cool and manicured right hand, Christian guessed Joan Randall had to be at least six feet tall in her heels. Six feet tall and more mesmerizing than any woman he had ever met.

As she looked at him, her dark eyes conveyed confidence, class, curiosity and maybe a hint of amusement. It was the "amusement" part that made Christian nervous.

She had seen right through him a few years ago. What was she seeing now, he wondered? More than that, "Why are you suddenly so concerned with what she thinks," Christian asked himself as she turned and walked to her chair at the table.

As she did and as he began to take his own seat at the head of the table, his eyes had taken her in again. She was wearing a cardinal red skirt and matching jacket with a white blouse underneath, which highlighted her tanned skin. Around her neck was a simple and elegant gold chain with a small gold crucifix hanging from the middle of it.

He hadn't seen her shoes, but he guessed the heels on them had to be at least four inches high.

***

As Joan sat at the highly polished mahogany table, she was equally surprised to realize that while she knew there were six other people in the room, she was really only aware of Christian Nicholas.

When she shook his hand, she noticed an immediate difference in him from the other time she had met him at the television studio. Now he seemed to be genuinely humble, genuinely contrite, and much more reserved.

***

While at first glance, he seemed even taller, more handsome, and more fit than she remembered, something powerful surely must have happened to him since their last meeting to transform him so, and she was more than happy to note the change.

***

Christian cleared his throat several times and all eyes turned toward him. As they did, his own eyes nervously looked back down at the pen before him.

"First, thank you all for coming on such incredibly short notice. My apologies for that. Next, one of you I just recently apologized to for my personal immature and selfish behavior..." His eyes shifted quickly to look at Joan and then back to the pen in front of him that he was still turning as a substitute security blanket. "The rest of you, in one way or another, I need to apologize to as well."

He took a quick sip of water from the glass before him before continuing.

"As all of you know to varying degrees, I made the last twenty plus years or so of my life all about me and my selfish and materialistic needs, and I hurt an awful lot of people in the process. An awful lot. Very good people who deserved much better from me. Well...life is nothing if not ironic. A few months ago, I woke up from a night of heavy drinking to find a note from my—as Page Six of the *New York Post* once described her—'twenty years younger than him trophy wife' saying that she was leaving me for her tennis instructor who was at least ten years younger than her. After I sobered up completely, I realized that the one and only emotion I was feeling was total relief. Total. The *New York Post* had been absolutely correct. I had only married Sandra for her looks, her figure, and the fact that she would look great on my arm. That was it. While she might be even more driven by materialism than I am, none of it was her fault. I now accept full responsibility for my empty and hedonistic lifestyle. In the days and weeks after finding the note, I did nothing but soul searching. Nothing. And what I realized was that I had turned into an ugly and shameful excuse for a human being. A waste of a human life. With each passing day after that, I began to hate myself more and more and between and during fits of despair, I began to contemplate the worst as a way to punish myself. But then...but then..."

Christian felt his emotions welling up and paused to compose himself before going on.

"But then, my older brother Paul called and literally saved my life. He *saved* my life. He is the minister at a good-sized church outside of Houston, Texas, and through my haze of self-hate, self-pity, and true disgust with myself for what I and I alone had turned myself into, he somehow found the words needed to reach me. The words needed to… *save* me. He knew I had been unhappy and miserable for decades and reminded me of the last time in my life I was truly happy. The *only* time I was *ever* happy. And that was when I was a little boy and the son of two parents in the United States Army who did not have two nickels to rub together as they sacrificed *everything* for their two sons. Paul reminded me that it was during those years that the birth and the message of Baby Jesus meant everything to me. That to honor His message of faith and hope, I began pretending to be Santa Claus to the children on the base who had lost a parent to war or who were even worse off than we were, that I was the most happy he had ever seen me in my entire life. Ever. And I knew…I truly knew…even through the haze of my pain and my darkest of thoughts, that he was absolutely correct. And then he spoke the words that saved me. My older brother Paul, the man of God from Texas said, '*Become a Santa Claus all over again.*' Seven words that I have been repeating in my head for days now. Seven words that I truly believe saved my life. Seven words that caused me to invite all of you here today. Seven words that made me see the light and see the mission I will now undertake for the rest of my mortal life. I believe that message came through my brother for a reason. I do. And for that reason, I *am* going to become a Santa Claus all over again. I am.

"When I was a small boy, I remember that my parents loved to watch Johnny Carson. A few years ago, I bought the entire *Tonight Show with Johnny Carson* DVD collection. Without a doubt, the most powerful moments ever televised from those shows was each Christmas season when Johnny Carson would read letters written to Santa Claus from desperately poor children. Each and every one of those letters shared one incredible and moving common denominator. *None* of those incredibly poor children ever asked Santa for a present or a toy for themselves. Ever. They *only* asked Santa to help their mommy, or their sister or their baby brother. *Never* themselves. They always said, '*whatever you might give me, please give to them.*' It is those children—those little angels on Earth—who I most want to reach. Who I most want to make smile. They will always be with us, and they will always put themselves last. Just thinking of such goodness and pure grace increases the shame I feel every day for the life I've led.

"Understanding all of that—if you are willing after you hear everything today—I *am* going to need each and every one of you to help me and in the process…bring at least some joy and some hope to such 'angels' and tens of thousands of poor and disadvantaged children around the world."

At that, Christian slowly looked up from the pen before him on the table, truly fearful of seeing the expressions on the faces of those before him. But what he saw changed…everything. What he saw was that all six of these highly accomplished and decent people were riveted by what he said. Three had tears in their eyes.

Seeing such an emotional and spontaneous reaction touched him deeply. Christian then looked around the table and made eye contact with the six people around him.

"Thank you," he softly said with the beginning of a smile of true happiness. "Thank you. Thank you all. Now…let me tell you of the crazy, impossible plan I have come up with."

CHAPTER EIGHT

"Okay," Christian said as he rubbed his hands together. "Two of the most valuable lessons I ever learned in life and business are first, it's generally better to ask for forgiveness than permission when looking to get something done, and second, that people tend to overly complicate tough assignments for their own reasons. Not that this isn't a *really, really, really* tough assignment…"

With that admission, Nicholas broke out laughing for a good twenty seconds. A laugh that was infectious rather than distracting.

Because of Christian's seemingly uncontrollable laughter, all those gathered at the table began to look at one another and smile while a few of them giggled at…well…they were not quite sure what they were giggling at, only that *his* warm laugh trigged their response.

Christian slowly stopped laughing in spurts as he used the backs of his hands to wipe his eyes when he realized he was going from one end of the emotional scale to the other in a matter of seconds.

"Sorry about that," he said with one last giggle. "Sorry. As mentioned, I have not slept much these last few days and I tend to get silly when I don't get enough sleep."

Ed Rogers, the very successful and powerful lobbyist from Washington, DC, lightly tapped on the table.

***

"No apology needed," began Rogers. "Laughter is the best medicine after all. So, with that in mind, how about you just cut to the chase here and tell us all what this *really, really, really* tough assignment is in case there might be a chance to laugh even more."

All those around the table with the exception of Christian and Rogers smiled as they nodded their heads in silent agreement. They had all been called here at the last minute for something important and were anxious to know the subject.

"Ed," answered Christian. "You're right. You're absolutely right. Okay. Here goes. I am, at times, a very literal person. Very. This is one of those times. My brother suggested I 'become a Santa Claus all over again' and I am going to do so in the most literal way possible. It is my intention…with your help or without it…but I truly and honestly hope and pray with it…to create…"

Christian took a deep breath before continuing. "…a real-life Santa's workshop at the North Pole and then for the rest of my mortal life here on earth, dedicate my time to making toys for those disadvantaged children around the world."

Not one person at the table laughed. Not one.

Instead, they all moved their chairs closer to the conference table and waited for Christian's next words.

***

"Leaving aside the myth and magic of the North Pole in this connotation," smiled Christian, "it's really just a construction project in a very tough environment. Well, Jeff and I…thanks to Ed opening the doors," he said, as he nodded his head toward the gray-haired but still baby-faced Rogers, "have completed a number of construction projects in very tough environments. Not the North Pole maybe…"

All those around him laughed with his words. But laughed, Christian could tell, in a supportive and interested way. As he quickly took in the faces, he was especially pleased to see that Joan's eyes seemed to be shining brighter than all the others with real interest in what had to seem to her, and to everyone else, like a truly crazy idea.

Christian next nodded his head toward Ed Rogers.

"Good old Ed here might have the toughest assignment of all. That being not only to get the blessing from the federal government to build this place, but then to keep it totally off the books and away from the prying eyes of the media."

"Is that all? Maybe we should rethink my fee," smiled the powerful Washington lobbyist as he shook his head back and forth.

Christian then turned and looked at the other attractive dark-haired woman in the room. That being his gate-keeper, most trusted aide, and senior vice president, Nina Sobhan.

"Nina. We are also going to need to draft a very short and very exclusive help-wanted ad. Maybe the most exclusive help-wanted ad of all time and when we're ready, place the ad in faith-based newspapers, magazines, and internet sites."

After making a note on her legal pad, she looked up at her boss and longtime friend and narrowed her hazel eyes.

"And who, exactly, are we hiring, Christian?"

Nicholas again stopped to look each person in the eye before settling back on Nina with a grin now spreading across his face.

"Elves. Honest to goodness elves."

CHAPTER NINE

After another hour or so of back-and-forth discussion, questions, and partial answers, the meeting concluded.

As everyone began to walk out of the conference room, Christian Nicholas hovered near the entrance. Just when Joan Randall was about to walk past him, he turned to face her.

"Joan. Do you have an extra few minutes to talk?"

She instantly broke into a smile which seemed even more powerful considering the contrast between her very white and very straight teeth, and her Florida-tanned face.

"Of course. I flew all the way up here with no notice because I was intrigued by you and the mission you hinted at. Now, after hearing you talk just a little bit more about it, I find myself amazingly excited with the idea of it all, and if it all makes sense, very anxious to be of help if I can."

Christian reclosed the door to the conference room and motioned Joan to the chair to the left of his at the head of the table.

As she nodded and walked toward it, he moved quickly to pull it out for her.

As he did, a smile reappeared on her face at his gesture of gallantry and good manners.

"Oh," stressed Christian as he pushed in her chair and then took his. "You can be of help. As a matter of fact, you might be the most important piece of this puzzle."

"How so?" she asked as she swiveled her chair to face him.

"First," Christian answered as he nodded his head toward a large assortment of coffee, juice, water, and sodas on a movable butler cart in the corner of the room. "May I get you a coffee, water, or a cold soda?"

Joan shifted her dark eyes from Christian, to the cart, and then back to Christian.

"Thank you, yes. I'd love a black coffee. But I can get it."

Before she could even finish the sentence, Christian had leapt out of his chair to get her coffee.

Twenty seconds later, he placed a fine white china cup of still steaming black coffee before Joan along with a small linen napkin.

"Thank you, Christian," Joan said with a warm smile and that hint again of amusement in her eyes.

"You're welcome," answered Christian in his deep voice as he contemplated what he had just done.

To most, Christian getting Joan her coffee would have been seen as evidence of the good manners of a gentleman. Christian mentally agreed with that but also could feel—much to his awakening curiosity and happiness—that the gesture was indeed, something a bit more. He was actually feeling a sensation that he had not felt since he was ten years old and had a crush on Debbie Anderson in the fifth grade.

Like that crush decades before, he was feeling…simple innocence and purity.

For his entire adult life, he had treated women as objects. He only cared about what *they* could do to make *him* happy. He rarely, if ever, cared about them or their feelings and emotions.

The shame he felt now for that selfishness and for those deeds hung around his neck like an anchor.

Today. Now. For the first time since that little crush on Debbie Anderson, he felt…clean. He felt excited about an innocence he had not felt in over four decades.

Suddenly, it was important to him to make a woman happy.

Suddenly, he needed the attention of Joan Randall. Suddenly, like a little schoolboy, he wanted her to know that he liked her. But not…for the first time in years…for him. He wanted her to know he liked her so she would be more open to letting him make her happy.

While it was still an alien feeling to him and he knew there was still a cleansing operation going on within him that would take a while longer to process, he also knew that every single time he made Joan smile, his heart would soar to a height it had never before attained.

Never in his deepest despair, did he ever dream that there existed a person—a woman—who could rediscover and bring out such feelings within him.

And yet, he thought, here I sit with a schoolboy crush.

***

Since she first blushed in the courtyard of her townhome in Boca Raton while speaking with Christian on the phone, Joan also realized that there was something more than simply business or charitable curiosity bouncing around in her mind.

Knowing that, she decided it best to be even more cautious than normal.

She took a sip of the hot coffee, gently placed it back on its saucer, then looked up at Christian who was looking at her with a smile.

"So…how can I be of help and why am I an important piece of the puzzle you are trying to put together?"

Christian shook his head very slightly as if trying to clear it and then instantly refocused on the massive undertaking he was about to embark upon.

"Well, as mentioned, you might be *the* most important piece of the puzzle."

"Why?"

"Because, when it's all said and done, our elves are going to need a place to live, work, eat, sleep, and socialize."

"Yes," Joan answered with a slight smile. "If you do manage to pull this all off, they will need just such a place."

Christian leaned over and slightly touched the back of her right hand with his fingertips.

"When *we* pull it off."

With his touch, it felt as if an electric current had run up her right arm.

Joan involuntarily jerked her hand back with his touch.

"Oh, I'm so sorry," Christian said as *his* face began to blush.

"No, it's quite all right," Joan said immediately as she looked down at her hand and then up at Christian's now worried face. "I'm not really sure *why* I did that."

"Well, I guess I do. I don't have the best reputation or track-record."

This time, it was Joan who reached over to touch the back of Christian's hand.

"Nonsense. You have been a perfect gentleman. Now...please continue."

Christian felt his face go warm again so dove right back into the conversation hoping the muted and soft lights of the conference room would hide his reaction.

"So...for us to pull this off, we are going to need a combination practical home and workplace for our group of elves, which should be about one thousand people at top capacity."

"One thousand," Joan said in shock.

"Well, eventually. Four to six hundred the first year or so, then we will slowly grow that number depending upon success."

Joan was still trying to wrap her mind around how one might house upwards of one thousand people in a secret location at the North Pole when Christian gave—and what should have been to her—the obvious answer.

"To accomplish this," continued Christian with now obvious excitement in his voice and mannerisms. "I decided the *only* logical thing to do was to, and this is the main reason I turned to you, is essentially place a cruise ship in and around the ice of the North Pole."

"A...a...cruise...a cruise ship," Joan began to stammer in response.

"Yes," answered Christian with a huge smile as he jumped up from his chair. "A cruise ship. And who better to help me with it than the former CEO of Carnival Cruise Line. Only *the* most successful cruise line in the world. Now if you don't mind, Joan, I have to run out to meet with my executive vice president."

"But..." Joan looked up at him with both confusion and curiosity filling her eyes.

"Joan," said Christian as he stepped back from the table. "If you are okay with it, I would love to continue this discussion tonight over dinner..."

"...A business dinner," Christian quickly added.

Joan laughed out loud.

"Well, if it's *only* a business dinner, then I will be happy to join you."

***

Fifteen minutes later, Christian was sitting in the office of Nina Sobhan. For the first fourteen minutes of that visit, he wrote on a yellow legal pad, crossing out some words, writing more, crossing out others until he was finally satisfied with what he had drafted.

All the while, with Nina looking on in a way that said, "I've seen this act before."

When he was finished, Christian tore the page out of the pad and slid it across the desk to her.

"There you go."

The woman who had been his most loyal employee, gatekeeper, and protector since the day he opened his firm picked up the paper, read his barely legible scratchings, and then placed it down before her.

"There I go, *what*?"

Christian jumped out of the chair as he began to turn toward the door.

"That's the ad I want to run in as many faith-based newspapers, magazines, sites, and blogs as possible."

"When?"

"Well…I want to send it tonight. When these faith-based editors and clergy open their computers tomorrow morning, I want this ad to be there. None of this is going to work if we don't start to identify our elves as early as possible. Elves who either do believe in the real meaning of Christmas, are seeking to be reconnected to that meaning all over again, or at the very least, want to help children."

Nina picked up the paper and read the words Christian had drafted then drew a box around:

HELP WANTED: If you love the true message of Christmas and wish to bring some joy to poor and disadvantaged children around the world and are willing to relocate to an undisclosed location and dedicate at least one full year of your life and be totally off-the-grid for that year, this job may be for you. But ONLY if you prepared to sign a nondisclosure agreement, go through a detailed screening process, and are truly serious about finding out more. If interested, please respond to this ad immediately.

"Christian," answered Nina as she stood up. "Two things. First, while I truly love and support the idea you've come up with, I hope you're not thinking of taking me with you, 'cause it ain't happening. I get scared going up one of those gondola things to the top of a ski slope in New Hampshire, let alone going to the top of the world at the North Pole. I'll be staying back here at the ranch keeping on top of things for you. And speaking of *that* duty, I'm not sending out anything until our legal counsel approves it."

"Okay," smiled Christian. "Well, first…you don't have to go. I'll feel better knowing you are back here protecting me as always. If we need a *Grinch*, I'll send for you. Next, I don't need Gerry's approval to write a simple little ad…"

"Christian…" said Nina in a stern voice while totally ignoring his attempt at humor.

"Nina…"

"Christian," she said again, drawing one of her well-known lines in the sand.

"Okay, okay. Have Gerry look at it and approve it. But he has to come here. We are not emailing this to anyone until it's ready."

"Fine. I'll have him come tomorrow."

"No," answered Christian in a firm, but not stern voice. "Now. Tonight."

"But he *just* left. He's back at his office in downtown Boston by now."

"So what?" said Christian with a slight laugh. "For what I pay him and his firm every year, he can make the forty-five-minute drive back out here right now."

"Alright," answered Nina as she sat back down to make the call. "I'll also have Marty come back in to create a protected email account that we can control for anyone who does respond."

"Right. Good idea. All of these elves *have* to be very good and very decent people. They have to be. That said, we all make mistakes in life—I should know—so I don't want to exclude anyone just because of something like that. In the next couple of days, let's perfect the screening process. One that is fair, but leaves no doubt that the applicants are the kind of people I want and need for this project."

Just as Christian was about to step out of her office, he turned to look back at her with a very serious look upon his face.

"Oh, and Nina. I need you to do something *very* important for me. When we do start screening and accepting applicants to become elves, I want you to pick out ten who will touch me in one way or another. You know me better than most after all these years so I totally trust your judgement on this. As much as possible, make it a cross-section of life experiences. Just real people. Once we have settled on those ten, I want to meet them as soon as it makes sense in terms of schedules and travel."

"Of course. I will make sure."

Christian stepped a foot closer to her.

"I know you will, but you have to *promise* me. It's very important to me that I sit down and talk with each of them."

Nina *did* know her boss better than anyone and knew when he needed absolute reassurance and honesty.

"Christian. You have my word, I promise."

"Great," he said as he clapped his hands together and walked out into the hallway.

CHAPTER TEN

At 7:00 PM that night, the town car that Christian had arranged to pick Joan up at her hotel dropped her off at Sophia's, a small, family run Italian restaurant on Main Street in Westwood.

Joan mentioned her name to the hostess who immediately began to escort her toward the back of the restaurant. As her eyes adjusted to the soft yellow lighting, Joan saw that the place was very retro in the sense that it could have been one of those always elegant restaurants they featured in 1940s movies.

Each table had a small white lamp with a red-and-white lampshade in the middle casting the yellow-white light, which added greatly to the ambiance. Each table also showcased Waterford crystal glasses and a full complement of silverware adorned the white linen and lace-trimmed tablecloths.

When they got to what Joan thought was the end of the restaurant, the hostess took a right turn and showed her into a small banquet room. There, she found Christian sitting at a table for four madly typing away into his smartphone.

As soon as he looked up to see her, a smile grew coast-to-coast on his face. He held up one finger to her, then typed several more characters, pushed "Send," and then put the smartphone in his pocket.

"Thank you, Anna," said Christian as he looked over at the young hostess standing next to Joan.

"You're welcome, Mr. Nicholas. Your waiter Dario will be here in a moment."

Christian rushed over and offered his arm to Joan for the ten-foot walk to their table. He then pulled out the chair at the far end of the table, which afforded the best view, and sat to her left.

Christian then looked over at Joan.

"Are you in a rush?"

Joan let out a small laugh as she shook her head.

"My schedule is yours."

"Wonderful," smiled Christian. "Then we will have an old-fashioned, leisurely dinner. The world and everyone in it is in too much of a rush. Time to stop and smell the roses."

He looked back at Anna.

"Anna, please have Dario give us ten minutes or so, then he can come and take our drink orders."

"Of course, Mr. Nicholas."

"They know me here," said Christian with his smile still in place.

"So I gathered," she smiled back at him as her eyes took in the banquet room. "It's really very quaint and quite elegant. Kind of a throwback."

"Exactly," answered Christian enthusiastically. "I don't know why, but even as a poor Army brat with nothing, I always loved those elegant restaurants in the old Cary Grant-Ingrid Bergman movies. Way before my time, but something about them always spoke to me. This place reminds me of those movies. The owners are an older couple from Rome. *Their* favorite movies are *Roman Holiday* with Audrey Hepburn and Gregory Peck and *Houseboat* with Sophia Loren and Cary Grant. So that tells you where *their* minds are at. That was their granddaughter Anna, who escorted you back here."

"I see. Do you like nostalgia?"

Christian shrugged his shoulders. "I guess I pick and choose like a lot of people. I mean, you never want to sound like your grandparents and start to spout, '*Back in my time,*' but sooner or later we all do, right? At least about some things. I've had this discussion with family and friends over the years, but if I could have picked a time period to be in my prime in the United States, I would have picked from 1945 to 1965. Those two decades for sure had a number of flaws, but at least to me, it was a simpler, more well-mannered, less hectic, better-dressed, and more faith-filled and patriotic time."

"Says the man," laughed Joan. "Who was just conducting business with his state-of-the-art smartphone when I walked into the room."

"Oh, don't get me wrong," responded Christian with a warm laugh. "I am not anti-technology. In some ways, I use more of it than anyone. In other ways, I think these 'smart phones' we all carry, are turning us into antisocial zombies as we stare mindlessly into their hypnotic white light."

Joan looked serious for a moment. "You might be surprised to hear that I completely agree with you. I have come to dislike and distrust the addictive power of those devices."

"Well, first. I am not surprised. And second—and this actually may surprise you—one of my favorite possessions in the world is a very old-fashioned black rotary-dial phone from 1946 that is in my home office."

"And do you morph into Sam Spade when you use it?"

"Ah," exclaimed Christian as he clapped. "A fan of Humphrey Bogart movies."

"Actually," said Joan as she shook her head. "A fan of Sam Spade. My dad used to be the chief of police for a small town in Illinois. When he was forced to retire because he reached the mandatory age, he hung up his own shingle as a private eye for a few years. Dashiell Hammett, the author of *The Maltese Falcon* and *The Thin Man*, was required reading in our house."

"Interesting. It's a very small and ironic world, indeed."

"Why," asked Joan as she picked up her crystal water glass capturing the light of the lamp before it.

"Well…and don't hate me…but I actually have first-edition signed copies of those two books."

Joan's dark eyes grew very wide.

"You have *first-edition* copies of *The Maltese Falcon* and *The Thin Man*—both of which, I think, were written in the 1930s—*actually signed* by Dashiell Hammett himself? They must be worth a small fortune."

"So my accountant tells me."

"Wow. I'd love to at least see them one of these days."

Christian went silent for a few seconds as he first, looked at the lamp and next took a sip of water before looking back up at her.

"Joan, instead of me letting you *see* them, would you allow me to give them to you?"

Joan sat back and more upright in her chair.

"*Give* them to me? Give me what are, in reality, priceless books... Christian, why would you do that? You don't even know me."

Christian looked down at the lamp again for a moment and then back into Joan's eyes, which were perfectly reflecting and framing the light.

"But that's just it. I may not have a logical reason for saying this but I actually *do* feel like I really know you. I do. For the first time in my life, I honestly and truly do feel that way."

Joan's mind started to go a million miles an hour with thoughts tripping over one another as they rushed to speak to her. Emotions she had not truly felt, *ever*, where now overwhelming her; she needed to tap on the brakes and think it all through.

Joan took a deep breath, let it out very slowly, and then looked at Christian.

"That's a very generous offer, but no. Thank you so much. I couldn't possibly accept them at this time. Now, you mentioned at the office that this was a 'business' dinner. Would you like to discuss your North Pole Project now?"

Completely undeterred, Christian latched onto her words "at this time," and afforded himself a slight smile before explaining in minute detail why placing the equivalent of an ultra-modern cruise ship in the ice and snow of the North Pole would be the perfect home for what he had designated as "*SW1*," for "Santa's Workshop One."

CHAPTER ELEVEN

Winston McNeil sat on a weathered green bench in St. James Park in the heart of London and stared mindlessly at the various birds gathered around his feet.

They were gathered there because over the years Winston and his beloved wife Diana had been the early morning buffet stop for the growing multitude of birds in the park as well as a fair share of squirrels.

For almost every day for the last three decades, Winston and Diana would leave their flat at five-thirty AM sharp for their two hour "constitutional," which would take them around Buckingham Palace, down past Whitehall, and eventually always lead them back to "their" bench in St. James Park.

Once there, they would happily take out their bag full of bread, break off little pieces and proceed to feed their "flock." For a number of reasons, Winston and Diana were not able to have children of their own and seemingly more by osmosis than anything else, they eventually mentally "adopted" the birds of St. James Park as their family, and had lovingly fed them almost every day for thirty years.

Today, as he had done for the last number of days, Winston sat on the bench and silently cried as he looked down at the birds looking up at him in anticipation and hunger.

For just over one month ago, he had lost his wife of fifty-two years to illness. For Winston, Diana was not just his wife and best friend on earth. She was his very reason for being. His *only* reason for being. Every day with her had been the best day of his life. Every day, he knew—only because of her—that the next day would be even better.

And now…she was gone.

And now…he was lost.

Winston sat alone on "their" bench and openly wept as he had done for the last few weeks. Now, he talked out loud to the birds and the squirrels and did not care in the least if the occasional early morning passersby thought him crazy or not.

"I don't know what to do," he said as he looked down at his feet as the tears flowed freely down his face and mucus began to drip from his nose. "I don't know what to do. My dear beloved Diana. I need you to tell me what to do. Please talk to me and tell me what to do. All of my adult life you guided me and were my foundation. I am so very lost without you and need you to guide me this one last time. Please talk to me now, my Diana."

Diana had always believed that people should dress as elegantly and as properly as possible. She had always believed deeply in manners, civility, and tradition and it made her quite sad over the years to see successive generations turn their backs on such basics. As she often told Winston, "No matter if you only have five pounds or five million, you should endeavor to dress your best while acting your best."

As he remembered that, Winston pulled a neatly folded handkerchief out of his crisp blue blazer and wiped his eyes and then his nose.

He carefully placed the handkerchief on the bench next to him and opened the bag of bread that had been resting on his lap for some minutes.

***

Just the sound of the paper bag opening had the birds quacking, squawking, and chirping away in excitement. As they hopped all around him fighting to be first to gobble down a piece of bread, Winston spoke aloud to them.

"She truly loved you all," he said with a forced and sad smile. "Our Diana truly loved you and cared about you."

Winston then shifted his gaze from the tens of birds on the path before him to a lone white cloud slowly floating past in the blue sky just above Buckingham Palace.

"Isn't that right, my dearest? As you always kidded me, the three loves in your life were me first, Christmas second, and our adopted family of birds, third. Well, here I am, sweetheart. I am here. For the last few weeks since you went up to Heaven, I have been out here feeding them. Can you see me? Can you? I do it for you. I do it because it's the last connection I have with you…I do it because…"

With that, Winston bowed his head as grief overtook him again.

With his head down and his frail body shaking slightly from the sobs, he did not notice a tall and very well-dressed young man in a dark three-piece suit walking on the path toward him from the direction of Parliament.

The man was about thirty years of age, had thick but short and expensively cut black hair, and was carrying a slim tan briefcase.

When he arrived at the bench where the older man was weeping, he stopped and gently put his right hand on Winston's shoulder.

"Uncle Winston," said the well-dressed younger man softly.

The older man ever so slowly looked up at the tall man who was now smiling down at him. As he did, confusion gripped his mind.

Recognizing that, the young man then knelt before the older man.

"Uncle Winston. It's me. Patrick. Patrick, your nephew."

Suddenly, the older man grabbed the handkerchief next to him on the bench and quickly wiped his eyes and nose again.

"Of course, it's you, Patrick," said the old man with the hint of a real chuckle. "I knew it was you. I know you're my nephew."

The fact was that his sister's youngest child was one of the true lights of his life. One was not supposed to have "favorites" when it came to nephews and nieces, of which Winston had five, but the truth was that ever since he was a little boy, Patrick had been the favorite both of him and Diana.

They had truly loved all of their two nephews and three nieces, but there was just something very special about little Patrick.

"Little Patrick," laughed Winston to himself as he looked at the now six-foot three-inch-tall man taking a seat next to him on the bench. A man who had excelled at sports, at Oxford, in business, and who now was one of the youngest members of Parliament in the House of Commons.

Just a few months before her passing, Diana had excitedly run into the living room waving that day's edition of their favorite newspaper, *The Daily Mail*. When she got next to her dear Winston, she proudly showed him an editorial from the paper stating that Patrick's political party was wisely grooming him to be a future Prime Minister of the nation.

"*Prime Minister*," Diana had whispered in unbridled pride.

Winston and Diana had almost immediately framed the editorial where it now hung proudly above Winston's desk in his home office, with another copy neatly folded inside Winston's wallet in his blazer pocket.

"How are you, Patrick," asked Winston as he turned his head to look toward Parliament and then back at his nephew. "Isn't your place of employment down the street there? A bit lost this morning, are you?"

Patrick's eyes lit up just seeing the older man. Since his mother and father had divorced twenty years earlier, Patrick had come to think of Winston as his surrogate father.

"Oh, I'm not lost at all, Uncle Winston. A bit upset that Crystal Palace lost two-nil to Man U last night, but other than that, I'm great."

Both Patrick and his Uncle were huge fans of the working-class Crystal Palace Eagles of the Premiere League and always tried to attend at least three or four home games per year.

"Well," smiled the older man, "once they get a few more English lads on the team, they will be fine. So…other than giving me the sports report, what brings you to our bench so early in the morning?"

"Actually," answered Patrick with a warm smile. "Maybe a prayer answered."

"A prayer answered?" asked Winston as his eyes narrowed in confusion.

Patrick turned on the bench to face the Uncle he loved so much. "I hope so. A couple of weeks ago, I sat down with my vicar to talk to him about you and the pain you've been in since…"

Winston's eyes instantly teared up again and Patrick gave him a few moments to gather himself before continuing.

"I explained to him that you have been so very lost and inconsolable these last few weeks and that I was afraid I might soon lose you as well."

Patrick was not surprised or remotely ashamed when his own eyes began to water with emotion.

"As the Vicar and I spoke, he asked me what Aunt Diana most cared about. I gave him your standard answer. 'My Uncle Winston, the true meaning of Christmas, and feeding the birds in St. James Park.'"

Patrick then put his hands on his uncle's shoulders. "Then, earlier this morning when I was having a spot of coffee and a biscuit, the vicar phoned me to tell me of a most unusual and somewhat mysterious ad that had popped up on the church website."

Winston was becoming more confused with each passing word. While he was truly warmed and comforted by the love and affection Patrick had for him, he was not remotely sure what his nephew was now talking about.

"What ad?" asked the older man. "What is this all about?"

"I am honestly not sure. But when the vicar saw the ad he told me his very first thought was of you. He said he had a vision of you, Aunt Diana, and Christmas. All together. When he called me, he read me the ad. Mysterious to be sure, but then…but then…I truly felt Aunt Diana's hand in all of this. I really did. So, if you are willing, I think it's something we need to explore right away."

The older man blinked back new tears as he reached for his nephew's hand. "Patrick. In mentioning your Aunt Diana, you just spoke the magic words. Tell me all about it."

CHAPTER TWELVE

Unlike a great many "billionaires" who were really *only* billionaires on paper because of the stock they either owned or controlled in their company, Christian Nicholas was an *actual* cash billionaire.

Back when he was a nine-year-old kid on an Army base collecting empty soda bottles for the deposit money, Christian decided then and there that "cash is king." He was no different now.

Almost all of his fifteen billion—and growing—fortune was in cash. With the "moderate" investment portfolios much of that cash sat in, Christian's accounting team told him if he did nothing for the rest of his life, absolutely nothing, he would make in the neighborhood of "one hundred million dollars per year, every single year, for as long as you live."

Of course, Christian was about to do the opposite of "absolutely nothing." The literally "polar" opposite of "absolutely nothing."

Back before his recent and life-changing "epiphany," Christian did indulge himself in as many "toys" as possible. Two of them being a six-passenger Learjet 70 and an eight-passenger, fully-loaded Gulfstream G650.

The Learjet 70 was for regional flights of 2,000 miles or less, while the Gulfstream G650 was more than capable of flying nonstop to most international destinations.

As Christian was contemplating the relative worth of a "huge amount of money," and how suddenly, "one hundred million dollars in interest per year" was now not nearly enough, he was seated across from Joan on his Learjet 70 on their way to a confidential meeting at the White House.

As a billionaire, Christian also strongly believed that the way one succeeded and, in fact, *grew* those billions, was to hire the best people possible in their respective fields to advise one along the way.

Ten years earlier, Christian realized that it could be quite lucrative handling projects for the federal government.

Unfortunately, there were already a great many firms ahead of him feeding themselves to the bursting point, at that taxpayer-funded trough.

Firms that were all part of the "Old-Boy" network of Washington, DC.

Other than going to the National Archives and the Smithsonian Air & Space Museum as a kid, Christian had not spent one moment in DC. As one of the largest taxpayers in the United States, the ever-growing pork barrel spending by Congress made his skin crawl on a regular basis.

Christian *was* a huge fan of classic movies and one of his all-time favorites was *Mr. Smith Goes to Washington* with Jimmy Stewart and Jean Arthur.

The movie, which dealt with the young, naïve, and newly appointed Senator Jefferson Smith having his ideals and faith in the U.S. government crushed into a fine white powder by DC insiders pulling the strings of certain members of Congress, was released in 1939. It was no surprise to Christian to learn that before the film was released, much of the Congress back then tried to have the movie—and its truthful message—banned.

To Christian's way of thinking, that same movie with the same villains could have been made today. Nothing had really changed. Neither political party really cared about the American people. Only about themselves and their own reelection.

Over the years, Christian liked to stress to friends, colleagues, and employees, "You have to be smart enough and honest enough to know what you *don't* know."

Christian knew beyond a shadow of a doubt that he knew *nothing* of the ways of Washington, DC, and would be instantly immersed in shark-infested waters should he try to dip his toes into what could be a highly lucrative, but highly guarded ocean of opportunity.

Knowing what he *didn't* know, Christian was determined to find *the* best person in Washington to help him navigate those waters.

After weeks of off-the-record conversations with well-connected friends, months of highly confidential research by some Harvard-trained analysts in his firm, and months pouring over the backgrounds of the very few names that did land on his desk, he finally found his perfect DC protector.

Not only was he the best government relations person in Washington, he was, by far, the best one in the country.

That was when he settled on Ed Rogers, a man who had easily forgotten more about Washington and government relations than most "experts" now claimed they knew.

Rogers was intelligent, calm, quiet, methodical, doggedly persistent, and zealously guarded confidences.

From a small town in Alabama, he had made himself a lawyer, and then from there, became a senior official in a winning presidential campaign, and then a senior White House official.

Because of his time in the White House, Rogers came to see how many corporations were being taken for a ride by firms who, oftentimes, did not have their best interests at heart.

Rogers also felt that at the same time, Congress and the White House were not getting the straight story on how and why the fate of corporate America was so critically important to the welfare of the nation.

Every four years and every presidential cycle, corporate America was vilified in the media as some, "evil monster out to hurt the little guy." To Rogers' point of view, if you subtracted the relatively few people in the executive-suite from the equation—some truly quite greedy and only interested in how much they could suck out of their company—"Corporate America" was in reality, the millions and millions of hardworking Americans employed by those firms who were making very moderate salaries indeed. Salaries they needed to live.

As Ed often explained, "Corporate America" is simply "our dads, moms, uncles, aunts, cousins, brothers, and sisters" working at a place that also happens to keep the "mom and pop stores in its orbit" in business.

As someone who ended up owning a number of these companies in his hedge fund, Christian very strongly agreed with that assessment.

Fifteen years earlier, Christian did acquire that small construction firm in Norwood, Massachusetts. Five years later, he found out that the U.S government was putting out a RFP (Request for Proposal) to build new U.S. embassies around the world that would be protected against terrorism.

Christian wanted to be in that business and that is when he tracked down Ed Rogers and eventually hired him.

Thanks to the hard and diligent work of Rogers setting up meetings with the right people, Christian's company not only got the contract, but the U.S. government saved millions when every embassy was finished well before the deadline *and* under budget.

From that contract came one that was completely off the books. It was a top-secret contract to build facilities for the three-letter agencies of the U.S. government anywhere in the country or the world where they needed to be built.

Christian's company now exceled at that task. Something that, along with the connections of Ed Rogers, Christian hoped could be leveraged in his favor as he explained *his* top-secret project to the White House.

CHAPTER THIRTEEN

Despite his great wealth and her former position as being one of the most successful and admired CEOs in the nation, neither Christian nor Joan had ever been to the White House before.

Both were now excited and neither one was ashamed to show it.

Because the meeting was highly confidential, they had entered the White House grounds via a black SUV with darkly tinted windows, that, after it had been checked and all the passengers screened by the Uniform Division of the United States Secret Service, had made its way up West Executive Avenue. Quite possibly—with all due respect to Downing Street in London—*the* most exclusive street in the world.

Situated between the West Wing of the White House and the Old Executive Office Building, which housed ninety percent of the White House staff, the street served a very important purpose. It kept visitors out of sight of the prying eyes of the media.

As Christian and Joan followed Ed Rogers into the ground floor of the West Wing, they made a very striking couple. Christian's six-foot three-inch-tall athletic frame was garbed in a black, hand-tailored suit over a crisp white French-cuff shirt with gold cufflinks, and a royal blue tie.

Joan, by a coincidence they had noticed on the corporate jet they had boarded in Norwood, Massachusetts, just three hours before, was also showcasing royal blue. In her case, it was a royal blue skirt and matching jacket over a white blouse with her ever-present gold cross hanging from its elegant thin gold chain around her neck.

They could have easily been taken for a Hollywood power couple.

As they waited to be cleared-in by the Secret Service on the ground floor of the building, several White House employees took immediate interest in Christian and Joan and nudged each other gently as if to silently say, "Wow. Who are *those* two?"

Both Christian and Joan were oblivious to the fact that they were having such an effect on those around them. Rather, both were mesmerized to realize they were *actually* standing in the West Wing of the White House.

"Wow," said Christian.

Ed Rogers turned his head to look at him. "Wow, what?"

"Wow," answered Christian as he waved his right hand before him. "That we are standing in the West Wing of the White House. Just amazing."

Ed Rogers paused to look around then looked back at Christian.

"Oh, yeah. I guess so."

"Well," laughed Christian. "Haven't *we* become jaded?"

"Give me a break, Christian," answered Ed with a smile. "First, I used to *work* here for four years, and second, my mind is totally focused on how we are going to convince the chief of staff to the President of the United States and his National Security Advisor to sign-off on your goofy little project."

"Oh, yeah," said Christian returning the laugh. "*That.*"

As if on cue, a young woman stepped out of an elevator just to their left to announce, "The chief of staff will see you now."

***

Christian, Joan, and Ed were escorted into the chief of staff's office, which, after the Oval Office of the President, was the most powerful and prestigious office in the White House.

Standing before them was Martha Sanders, the chief of staff along with retired general David Hunter, the President's National Security Advisor.

As soon as they walked in, the chief of staff gave Ed Rogers a warm hug. It turned out, before she became the campaign manager for the

President's campaign, she had been a vice president in Rogers's lobbying firm.

After everyone shook hands and introduced themselves, Sanders looked at Christian and Joan with a smile as she pointed to Rogers.

"Whatever you do, don't *ever* play golf with this guy. He'll end up with the keys to your car and your home."

"*Now* you tell me," answered Christian. "Unfortunately, I *have* played golf with him and the only reason I come to see him now is to visit what *used* to be my money."

Martha Sanders laughed as she escorted them all to the conference table in her office, and after coffees and water were poured, addressed them.

"Mr. Nicholas. Ed came in just the other day to give us at least *some* the confidential background regarding your project. To put it mildly, it's the most unusual request we have ever had."

"Ms. Sanders. General Hunter," began Christian as he looked at two of the most powerful public servants in the nation. "Thank you so much for seeing us on such short notice. Before I make my pitch, however, I'd like to introduce Joan Randall."

"Oh," smiled Sanders. "No need to introduce her."

She then turned her face to look at Randall.

"Not that you are that much older than me, but in all honesty, you have been a role model of mine for a very long time. Carnival Cruise Line was already an exceptional company. But what you did with it after you became CEO was truly incredible. About seven years ago, you gave a speech about the importance of women not only reaching the C-Suite, but becoming CEOs and addressing the needs of corporate America based upon *a woman's* real-world experience and perspective. I was in the front row for that speech, and I may have actually bought the first ticket to the event."

"Well, thank you for saying that, Ms. Sanders…"

"Martha, please…" jumped in Sanders with a smile.

"Thank you…Martha," nodded Joan. "All I can tell you at the moment is how honored I am to meet both you and General Hunter."

"Well…" continued Sanders as she looked over at Christian. "To be quite honest, one of the main reasons Mr. Nicholas got this meeting— with *no* notice," she stressed as she smiled and stared at Rogers, "was because Ed told us you were part of the team."

"*Now*, will you take those books?" asked Christian with a smile as he looked at Joan.

"What?" said Ed Rogers.

"Sorry," answered Christian with a sheepish grin. "Inside joke."

"This is the White House, Christian," said General Hunter with a chuckle. "No inside jokes allowed. You will now have to tell us the story…but only *after* you try to sell us on your project."

CHAPTER FOURTEEN

"Thank you, General Hunter, thank you Martha, and thank you Ed, for setting up this meeting...with *no* notice."

Christian paused for just a few seconds to collect his thoughts before continuing.

"Martha and General Hunter. You know me, or more accurately, know *of* me, because of the professional relationship my construction firm has had with the U.S. government for the last decade. What you may not know, is that until very recently, I have been a miserable excuse for a human being..."

"Christian," interrupted Rogers. "There is no need for you..."

Christian held up his hand.

"Ed. It's okay. It really is. I'm about to ask a lot from these people and they deserve to know everything. More than that, it's their right."

Christian picked up his small white coffee cup trimmed in gold and noticed the seal of the President of the United States embossed on the outside, also in gold.

Just seeing that symbol, which reminded him that he was, in fact, sitting in the home of all the American people, convinced him all the more that he was doing the right thing.

"As I was saying," Christian continued after taking a sip of his coffee and putting the cup back down. "The truth is, I *have* been a miserable excuse for a human being these last four decades or so. There was no one more selfish, no one more hedonistic, and no one more superficial than I was. Not too long ago, I was sitting in my home office. I had not bathed in days. I had not talked to anyone in days. I had hit rock bottom. I had every material thing in life a person could ever dream of, and yet, I had nothing. *Nothing.* Life didn't seem worth living anymore. But just as I had come to that conclusion, my older brother from Texas called. He is a minister, and through the haze of my self-hate, he somehow got through to me. He somehow showed me the light. He reminded me of the one time in my life, when I was but a little boy, that I was truly *selfless* and truly happy. It was when I, as a child, saved money to buy toys for other kids on the Army base where we lived who needed them more than I did. It was that act of giving that made me happy. Making others happy, made *me* happy. It truly did. It gave me a purpose. Then after four decades of shaming myself with my behavior, my brother Paul—minister Paul— simply told me, '*Become a Santa Claus all over again.*' And as I have a very literal mind, that is exactly what I intend to do."

"Literal," said the chief of staff. "In the sense that you want to do something at The North Pole. At least…that's what Ed mentioned."

"He is correct. But much more than 'something,' Martha," answered Christian with a nod of his head. "I want to do something *permanent.*"

"Permanent," exclaimed the general as he exchanged looks with the others at the conference table.

"Yes, sir. Permanent," said Christian with a slightly harder edge to his voice. "With all due respect sir, in many ways, our world is becoming less safe, more uncertain, and sadder by the day. Much more. Not only are more people falling into poverty, but more and more people are simply losing faith in…*everything.* They are losing faith in governments, employment, the future, each other, and…*faith* itself. Even the ultra-wealthy—as they wall themselves off from humanity—are losing faith. No matter how much they try, and I am an expert on this subject, the emptiness they now feel can never be filled with material goods or selfish pleasures. And at the end of the day, when they look through their bleary and bloodshot eyes into the mirror at what they've become, they know that more than anyone. They know the truth."

"And with what you are proposing, Christian?" asked Martha Sanders. "Do you think you are going to solve that problem?"

"Not even close, Martha," answered Christian with a laugh. "Not even a dent, really. And I know that. Look, ultimately, and for sure, all of us at this table know this, we will never solve the world's problems associated with poverty and misery in a macro sense. Never. But what we *can* do, every one of us in our own way, is improve the life of at least *one* of our fellow human beings who is suffering. We truly can. And, as my brother reminded me, because of the wealth and the bit of power I have accumulated over the years, I have the ability to help quite a few people—poor and disadvantaged children, mostly—for the rest of my natural life."

"That honestly does sound wonderful," said the thirty-eight-year-old chief of staff. "It really does. But why the North Pole? Pardon me, but that *does* sound a bit…eccentric. You can set up all kinds of charities all over the United States and all over the world."

Christian nodded his head as he took a quick look at Joan and shot her a wink.

As Christian began to answer the chief of staff, Joan felt her face flush anew because of the wink.

"Yes, I can. I guess I am picking The North Pole for three main reasons. First, because I *am* a very literal person and if I'm going to 'become a Santa Claus' all over again, what better place than the North Pole to carry out that mission. Next, I guess I picked the North Pole because somewhere deep inside, I'm a romantic at heart. While that feeling and reality has been buried deep within me for decades, it seems to have surfaced…of late."

With that statement made, Joan took an immediate and intense interest in studying a small wrinkle on the napkin before her with the seal of the President in its middle.

"And last," continued Christian with now a self-knowing grin on his face. "I guess I picked the North Pole because I can. The inner-child in *me* likes the idea. Me. I *want* to go there. It gives me a challenge. It doesn't have to make sense to anyone else. It makes sense to me.

"At my firm, I have some of the best analysts in the world, and what they tell me is that in-fact, no nation on earth 'owns' the North Pole. No one. No nation and no person has sovereign rights to the North Pole. Five nations—Russia, Canada, Norway, Denmark (via Greenland), and the United States—are, at any time, engaged in active debate about this subject, but none can claim anything. All five of these 'Arctic Surrounding' nations are allowed exclusive economic zones which extend two hundred nautical miles from their coasts toward the North

Pole. But *none* have any authority over the North Pole or who goes there. Not even the government of the United States."

"If that is all true, Christian," said General Hunter, "and I *will* look into the subject further to be sure, then why do you need us?"

"Well, because I want your help and…your cover."

"Our cover?" said the Chief of Staff as she shot Ed Rogers a worried look.

Christian held up his hands.

"Honest. It's not that complicated and well within your power to make happen. But, before we get into any of that, may Joan explain some of the logistics involved in all of this."

CHAPTER FIFTEEN

"Of course," answered Martha Sanders. "I am looking forward to her thoughts on all of this."

"Me, as well," smiled Christian.

"Well," began Joan as her dark eyes lit up with the task before her. "My instant reaction when I first heard the idea, was that Christian maybe lost his mind…"

"Don't sugarcoat it, Joan," said Christian. "I can handle the truth."

After everyone stopped laughing, Joan went on.

"But…" she stressed, "the more I heard him speak about it—and we talked about it for two hours last night and another two hours on the flight down here—the more I came to believe that it was the *sanest* and most wonderful idea I have ever heard."

"Thank you," said Christian in a voice just above a whisper.

"You're welcome," said Joan as she now involuntarily reached over and touched the back of his hand.

Ed Rogers, Martha Sanders, and General Hunter all shared a quick look of curiosity at the small gesture of affection.

"Christian is absolutely right," continued Joan. "We will never solve poverty, misery and loneliness on a macro level. Ever. But we all *can* make a difference. We all can help someone. One, five, ten or a few hundred at a time. We can. If I may, what Christian has decided to do is not only exceptional and unprecedented in its scope, but incredibly unselfish. He has decided that with the time he has left on earth—and with

God's blessing let's hope that's at least another thirty years—to spend *his* billions of dollars—not one tax dollar—*only* helping to deliver toys, food, medicine, books, and happiness to what will amount to millions of poor and disadvantaged children all over the world for the next few decades. He is not leaving his money to some college where it might be wasted. He is not leaving it to some charity only to see most of it spent on salaries, lavish trips and overhead with only a tiny percent going to those intended. He is not agreeing to build symphony hall for a city but *only* if they name it after him in fifty-foot high letters. No. He is going to use his billions to directly help poor, disadvantaged and abandoned children."

Christian cleared his throat.

"Okay. Thank you again, Joan." Said the now slightly self-conscious Christian. "Thank you," he added as he looked at her with a smile of real gratitude. "Let me say something else, and then we can get back to you talking about the *logistics* of it all."

He then looked from Ed Rogers to Martha Sanders to General Hunter.

"Ed knows this, but I want both of you to know as well. For me, there *is* a spiritual part to all of this. There is. In terms of faith, I truly lost my way and I'm trying to find my way back. For me, that means speaking to Jesus again. For me, that means seeking His forgiveness for the life I've led. For me, that means putting '*Christ*' back into Christmas. It truly does. To me it does seem nonsensical, sad, and more than a little worrying that when Christmas does show up on our calendar—a day originally *only* celebrated to honor the birth of the Baby Jesus—some want to turn 'Christ' into a secular word while those who do still honor Him on that day, are sometimes scared to even say '*Merry Christmas*' out of fear of offending someone. Again, for me, Christmas is about Christ. Hence the name '*Christ*mas.'

"But I want to stress something. That is only *my* opinion. *No one* will be forced to share it and no one has to agree with me. No one. *Period.* Anyone can help. It will be wonderful if you do believe in the true meaning of Christmas, but not mandatory at all. No matter if you believe or not, if you want to help children and make a real difference, and are a very good and decent human being, then that is all that matters to me personally. The children I intend to help live—no, *barely* exist—in many countries around the world. Some of those countries are majority Christian. Many are not. It doesn't matter. It's the desperately poor children in those countries that matter to me. Christian, Jewish, Muslim,

Hindu, Buddhist, it does not matter. They are *all* God's children and are *all* deserving of at least some fleeting moments of happiness in lives so tragic, most of us could not possibly imagine."

Without even realizing it, Martha Sanders' eyes began to water as she thought of her twelve-year-old son and seven-year-old daughter and how very fortunate they were.

Christian didn't want to depress anyone. He simply wanted them to understand *his* personal motivations, understand the situation, understand the need, and to truly understand that it was his intention to do something about it.

"Okay," Christian said with a real but calculated smile. "Enough of the sappy stuff. If it's okay with Joan, maybe *now*, she can tell you about some of the logistics involved and stop making up nice things to say about me."

"I'll try," said Joan as she then winked back at Christian.

"How *long* have you two known each other?" asked Ed with a grin.

Christian wrinkled his forehead. "What does that have to do…"

"Oh, nothing. Just curious," answered Ed as he looked at Martha and General Hunter who had not caught the wink. "Joan. Please continue."

"Alright," began Joan a little awkwardly. "Alright. So…logistics. Well, again, Christian and I have spoken quite a bit about this. Without *'making up nice things to say about him,'* I do have to stress that all of this was his idea. In a good way. Meaning, no matter if he wants it or not, he does deserve the credit. He reached out to me because of my past career. Something Martha was so nice to mention a short while ago."

"You mean being the CEO of Carnival Cruise Line?" asked the Chief of Staff.

"Yes. In what is turning out to be a remarkably short time period, Christian truly did think all of this through. Now, will some think it fanciful, silly, child-like or even crazy that he has decided to base his operation on The North Pole? Some will. Martha, you touched upon it a few minutes ago. Both you and the General might be having those exact thoughts—or worse—right this moment. And that's okay. The fact is, The North Pole *is* the place Christian selected and as a former—hopefully successful—CEO, I know well that when the big boss or the board make a final decision on something, then it's up to the executives and staff to make that vision and goal a reality.

"As Christian said before, the construction company he owns has built highly confidential complexes for the United States Government in some very inhospitable places. Not The North Pole, but in a few cases, even more challenging. As you may know, The North Pole is in reality, just one giant ice flow or series of ice flows connected to each other off and on. It is *not* land. At any given time, it's about the size of the United States give or take the winter freezing and the summer warming. The closest land to The North Pole is in-fact, straight down about 14,000 feet at the bottom of the Arctic Ocean. In the winter, the average temperature is about minus 40 degrees Fahrenheit. In the summer months, the temperature can rise as high as 32 degrees Fahrenheit. In the winter, the sun is never seen. In the summer, it never sets. The ice pack that makes up The North Pole can be from three to twelve feet thick. The constants being frozen-ice, melting ice, nonstop movement, and…water. Lots and lots of water.

"If you wanted to set up shop on The North Pole for just the winter, then you could build something on the ice pack. But…if you wanted to be up there year-round, then you're going to need a…"

"A ship," said Martha with a smile.

"Exactly," nodded Joan. "A ship Christian has designated as '*SW1*.' But not just any ship. Given the needs and parameters of the mission Christian has articulated, we are going to need…"

"A cruise-ship." said General Hunter.

"Precisely," answered Christian jumping back in the discussion. "Recently, a senior vice president in my firm sent out maybe the most unique 'Help Wanted' ad ever drafted. An ad, which, as we speak, is continuing to pop up in a number of on-line faith-based newspapers, web-sites and blogs around the world."

"Why is it unique," asked Martha. "Who are you trying to hire?"

Christian looked at Joan, then Ed, then the General, and finally back at the Chief of Staff.

"Elves."

CHAPTER SIXTEEN

"Alright," said General Hunter, with a look of frustration now clearly showing on his face. "With all due respect, this really *is* starting to sound rather silly...and we really *do* have a White House to help run."

Christian then got help from an unexpected ally.

"General Hunter," said Martha Sanders as she nodded to Christian and Joan before looking at the General. "Instead of 'Elves,' simply change the name to 'staff' or 'employees.' Instead of *The North Pole*, imagine a factory being built on the snow-covered plains of Montana. Would it sound 'silly' then for an American businessperson or entrepreneur to do such a thing? I don't think so. I believe we—and I include myself in this criticism—are falling into a trap created by our imaginations fed over the years by movies, books, and stories about Santa Claus and the North Pole. Wonderful stories for some of us for sure, but stories which turned the North Pole into a mythical place. But, as Joan just rightfully pointed out, it's simply an ocean of frozen ice at the north pole of our planet. It's just a place. So, if we can successfully remove the mythical from our thinking process, then it's just another tough place to work. And, once again to Christian and Joan's point, if you are going to operate a project year-round in that unforgiving environment, then you will need a ship. A ship that can house, feed, and medically care for the 'staff' or 'employees' you intend to hire. 'Staff' or 'employees' who will need a place to..."

Martha turned to face Christian.

"Make toys," said Christian, turning his gaze to the general. "Basic toys for children with nothing. Will it solve the problems of the world? No. Will it bring some happiness to—the first year—tens of thousands of children? We hope so. Because along with the toys, as Joan mentioned, we are also going to deliver food, books, medicine, and the message… depending upon the country…of the true meaning of Christmas."

General Hunter slowly shook his head.

"Alright. Assuming I buy into Martha's example and now think to myself that this is just another businessperson building a facility in a tough area and then housing 'staff' in that facility when it's ready, I still need to understand what you want from us."

"Cover and help."

"Christian," said Martha. "You already said that. What exactly does it mean?"

"Two things. First, we are going to need an ice-breaker from the U.S. government. Something to clear the way for the ship we have picked out…."

"Wait a minute," interrupted Ed Rogers with a surprised look on his face. "You *already* have a ship picked out? How is that possible?"

"Actually," answered Joan. "It's really fairly easy. When I was with Carnival, we worked with an exceptional ship builder in Italy by the name of Fincantieri. As it turns out, they are just finishing a 2,000-passenger cruise ship for a company that just went bankrupt. So…"

"So," said Christian with a smile. "I bought it."

"What…you bought…when?" stammered Ed Rogers.

"On the flight down here."

"On the flight down here," exclaimed Rogers. "*When* did you two meet again?"

"Luckily for you, only about a week ago. Had we been planning for a full month, we'd be telling you of our plans to take over the world."

Everyone laughed except General Hunter who simply looked over at Martha Sanders and offered her a small frown before continuing.

"Christian. Can we go back to the ice-breaker request and the cover you mentioned?"

"Yes, sir. Sorry for the joke."

"Oh, no." smiled the General. "Jokes are fine. No apology needed. I like a good joke as much as the next person. But what I like even better than a good joke are rational reasons for a most unusual request."

"Yes," smiled Christian in return. "You are right. In this particular case, that is *much* better than a good—or even marginal—joke. So with regard to the ice-breaker, it's the answer you have already guessed. We need it to clear the way for our ship…"

"*SW1*," added the chief of staff who was clearly warming to the whole idea and project.

"Yes," nodded Christian. "*SW1*…for 'Santa's Workshop One.'"

As he said that, he stole a quick look at the general who was compressing his lips while biting his tongue.

"…Beyond that," Christian continued. "We would like your assistance to keep the whole thing secret. During the journey and most certainly when on station at the North Pole, *SW1* will be camouflaged to mirror its surroundings. No sense in any private or government satellites getting photos of this project and putting it on the web. As I will be funding every single penny of this—including reimbursing the expenses of the U.S. government for the services of the ice-breaker—it does not have to be on the books. In fact, if any cover story is needed, you could simply say the U.S. is setting up a small drift weather station."

"You really have thought of everything," said Martha Sanders with some real admiration.

"No," answered Christian as he shook his head. "With each passing day, we will find issues which need to be addressed. New and unexpected questions which must be answered. Most having to do with *SW1*. But that is one of the many reasons why Joan is *the* key part of this team. As I think you know, Martha, she worked her way up through every conceivable job in the cruise industry. Both on the ships and then as an executive. One of her most important roles being as the Hotel Manager on several ships. That knowledge and skill-set are priceless, and I am very lucky to have her with me on this project."

"Thank you, Christian," said Joan softly.

There were several seconds of silence before the chief of staff spoke.

"First. Yes, Christian. You *are* very lucky to have Joan Randall on your team. If this goes forward—with or without our help—that will be an understatement. Next, if you don't mind, I would like to raise this issue with the President. When I have an answer, I will get back to you."

"That would be wonderful," answered Christian. "When do you think that might be?"

"Depending on the President's schedule, no later than tomorrow afternoon. I will call you then…one way or another."

***

Later that evening, after a debriefing meeting at the office of Ed Rogers on 13th Street, Christian and Joan found themselves seated at a corner table of the rooftop patio of the Hay Adams Hotel ironically enough, directly across Lafayette Park from the White House with an unencumbered view of one of the most iconic office-residences in the world.

Christian stared across the park at the White House bathed in a series of soft white lights, for several seconds before turning his head to look at Joan, who was focused on him.

"Interesting day," she said as she smiled over the rim of her glass of white wine.

"Interesting last number of days," Christian answered as he reached across the table and once again touched the back of her hand.

Christian was pleased—and encouraged—when she didn't instinctively pull it away as before.

"Joan," began Christian again as he pulled his hand back. "Do you believe people can truly change later in life?"

"You mean, can a leopard really change its spots kind of question?"

Christian slowly nodded his head up and down as he studied her face and eyes.

"*Exactly* that kind of question. Maybe even substitute *weasel* for leopard. And let me answer my own question first. I honestly never thought so. I've been around an awful lot of ah…weasels in my life—including one who leered at me every morning from the mirror—and one thing became very predictable about them. That being they *were* predictable. You could mostly always expect them to do the worst and almost always *only* care about themselves. Sadly, and now to my great shame, I was often holding the baton and leading that parade of self-indulgence and depravity."

Joan took a slow, deep breath as she tried to corner the least raw and most rational thought of the many raw and conflicting thoughts overtaking her mind.

The one that pushed itself instantly to the forefront was that *this*, Christian's vulnerability and brutal honesty about his past flaws and sins, was why he had suddenly touched her and why he was suddenly beginning to speak to her as no other had before.

As a very high-profile CEO, she had been around every "Type A" personality there was. Many who thought "superficial," "cruel," and "arrogant" were strengths, compliments, or goals yet to attain. Not one of them ever had an introspective "could I be the problem" moment in their lives.

Christian, on the other hand, seemed determined to atone for all of them.

And as he did so, quite sincerely and with great remorse in her opinion, he became all the more endearing to her.

There truly was a childlike quality to it all. Something that was now framing Christian in a whole new light.

"Well," she began with her thoughts now more organized. "While I tend to agree with you about weasels changing their spots, they have exceptions to every rule for a reason. My instincts are telling me that you *might be* just such an exception."

Christian looked at her for several seconds before turning his head slightly to look at the illuminated White House, and then back at Joan.

"Thank you," he finally said. "Interesting day, for sure."

He then pulled his right coat sleeve up just an inch so he could see his watch.

"Yikes," he exclaimed. "It's late. Our jet is wheels up back for Massachusetts at 7 AM."

"Oh, you poor baby," answered Joan with a full laugh. "You have to get up early to get on your own multimillion-dollar private jet."

"Oh, yeah," laughed Christian in return. "Does that sound spoiled? Do you think I'm spoiled? *Is* that spoiled?"

Joan held her thumb and index finger an inch apart.

"Maybe just a tiny bit."

"Could be. Could be," as he tried to affect a contrite face. "Well, look, when we are at cruising altitude, I'll only have *one* espresso instead of my usual two. Does that help?"

"Wow. Your willpower and willingness to do the right thing are inspiring."

"Yes, I know," he laughed. "I do it for the little people."

Joan bowed from her seat.

"And we *all* appreciate it, your highness."

"Then all is once again right with the world," smiled Christian as he stood. "Now, may I escort you to your room?"

"I would be honored, kind sir."

***

True to her word, less than twenty-four hours later, Martha Sanders placed a call to Christian who was now back in his office in Westwood, Massachusetts.

"Hello," said Christian after the call was put through to him by his assistant.

"Good afternoon, Christian. It's Martha Sanders."

"Thank you for getting back to me so quickly, Martha," said Christian in as calm a manner as possible while inside, nervous anticipation was already taking over his body.

"Well," began the chief of staff. "All unofficially and in complete confidence, the President seems to love your idea. Thinks that what you will be doing for these children is incredibly generous and heartwarming. That said, the President did have *one* stipulation to you getting our 'unofficial cover and cooperation.'"

Christian let out the long breath he did not realize he was holding.

"Of course. What might that be?"

"Well, since *you* brought it up, the President thinks that you should then have a real U.S weather monitoring team housed at *SW1*. Permanently. It would certainly add to the narrative and the cover."

"I will be honored to house the team and pay the expenses if needed."

"Well...in that case...congratulations. You will have our unofficial cooperation."

"Thank you, Martha. And from me to you, thank you so much for the kindness you showed us yesterday."

"Christian. Like the President, and speaking as a mother, I love the idea of what you are doing and the joy your North Pole Project will bring to so many desperately needy children around the world."

"Thank you, Martha."

"You are most welcome. Oh, and Christian..."

"Yes?"

"...I was *not* kidding. The President truly loves the concept of this project. So don't be surprised if when you are up and running, the President decides to pay you a visit and maybe help build a few toys for the children."

"Nothing would make me prouder, Martha. I would be speechless if that day came. Please thank the President for me."

CHAPTER SEVENTEEN

Jose and Anita Gomez held hands as they walked through one of the poorer neighborhoods in Mexico City. After forty-four years of marriage, they were still deeply in love and were truly each other's best friend in life.

They had never had much in terms of money or material possessions, but for them, they had more than enough. For Jose and Anita, strong family and strong faith were everything and they were blessed to have both. They raised their two beautiful daughters in a less-than-modest, tiny two-bedroom home that had a roof that constantly had to be repaired. But that, and the other hardships in life they endured, paled in comparison to their overall happiness.

Jose worked as a senior groundskeeper at the golf course of a luxury hotel two miles from their home. A job to which he had walked back and forth, six days a week, for twenty-seven years.

Because of his job and because of the oftentimes harsh necessities of life, he had become very good with his hands. As such, he tended to fix anything and everything that needed fixing. Including a leaky roof from time to time.

As they walked home from mass on an early Sunday morning—and the only day off per week for Jose—Anita brought up a subject she raised at least once a month for the last year.

"Jose," smiled Anita as she tugged on her husband's hand to get him to stop walking.

"Yes, *mi vida*," replied Jose as he returned the warm smile of the woman who had become his entire life.

"You *know* what," Anita answered as she laughed softly.

"You want to talk again about our needing some mission in life now that our girls have both married and are living in the United States?"

"Yes," answered Anita as she looked into her husband's sixty-four-year-old eyes. "I want to talk about that."

Jose shrugged his shoulders. "But I told you, *mi corazon*. If you find such a mission for us, then the answer for me is simple. I will do it. My place is with you."

The smile on Anita's face grew much wider as she opened her purse and took out the small weekly church newspaper.

As his wife opened the paper and began turning the pages in growing excitement, Jose looked upon her with pure pride and love. He knew his life was made whole when he had met her over four decades earlier.

When she found the page she was looking for, she stepped closer to Jose and leaned against his still strong body.

Jose hugged her with his left arm as he looked down at the newspaper.

"And what am I looking at, my wife?"

"This," she said as her smile grew even wider as she pointed at a small advertisement on the bottom right-hand side of the paper.

Jose laughed as he reached into his shirt pocket for his reading glasses. "I need my extra-eyes to read words so small."

As he began to read the words in the ad, his eyes opened more and more in amazement, curiosity, and a certain amount of disbelief.

"But," said Jose as he looked down at his wife's now childlike face. "This has to be a joke. Someone is playing a joke on the people of our small church."

Anita strongly shook her head as her smile continued to spread across her still beautiful face. "It is not a joke, my husband. I asked Father Miguel and he told me the ad is real. He told me that it is an ad being run in a number of faith-based newspapers and sites around the world."

Jose stared at the ad without blinking. "It's real? You are sure?"

"Yes, my husband. I am sure."

"And you...you...want us to do this crazy thing?"

"Yes, I do," she answered as she squeezed her husband's arm. "More than anything else at the moment. This...this is our mission. I am sure of it."

"But," said Jose as he laughed. "You admit it's beyond crazy."

"I do," she answered as she nodded her head. "I know it's crazy. But I also know it's a leap of faith we were meant to take *together*."

"Then," answered Jose as he folded his wife into his loving arms. "We will do so, together as always."

CHAPTER EIGHTEEN

Over the course of the next couple of weeks, Christian, Joan, and the team worked almost nonstop to try to figure out the step-by-step process needed to make Christian's "flight of imagination" idea into a full-blown reality.

While Christian tended to be a "make it up as you go along" person, Joan was much more detail oriented. Much more organized. Much more anal. One piece had to be plugged in after the previous. It had to make sense.

Part of what made Christian the massive financial success he had become over the last couple of decades was that he didn't believe he had to play by the rules all the time. He often thought the rules were invented by the "non-dreamers" and the conformists to keep the "Dreamers" and the "Doers" from leaving them in their dust.

All through elementary school and high school, Christian had been a dreamer. He would constantly gaze out the school windows at the blue sky outside and the clouds floating by and simply wonder, "Why?" and "What if?"

After college and fresh into his financial career, he quickly realized that you did have to pound some square pegs into some round holes from time to time. Not everything in business or in life fit as perfectly as many had hoped.

Business was imperfect and life was imperfect because people were imperfect.

If the square peg fit into the square hole, good for you. But if it didn't and you were really up against it and a massive deal—or your very job— was on the line, what then?

Conform or pound?

Christian would pound the wrong peg into the wrong hole every time versus doing nothing.

Now, as Joan watched him think, create, and solve problems, she came to believe that Christian was brilliant. But she also understood that it was a brilliance that had to be channeled. Had to be directed.

She had a tiger by the tail in Christian and knew she was in for the ride of her life.

As that thought crossed her mind, so did an image of her sister Janice's smiling face. A smile which said, "This is the one. This is why you waited. Sometimes things *do* happen for a reason."

Joan smiled with the thought of her sister's smile then quickly shook her head.

A head she knew, that *had* to get back in the game.

At that moment, it meant trying to imagine how the cruise ship Christian had just bought would look when reconfigured into *SW1*.

The good news was that Joan knew the design of the ship well. It was a "Vista Class" ship. The same class of ship Holland America used for its Ms. *Eurodam,* Ms. *Westerdam,* Ms. *Nieuw Amsterdam,* and a few others. The same design Cunard used for its *Queen Victoria* and *Queen Elizabeth.*

As Carnival Cruise Line was owned by Carnival Corporation, as was Holland America, Cunard, Princess and a few others, Joan had been able to sail on a number of Vista Class ships while in training and even on a few during semi-work-related vacations.

By great and good coincidence, it happened to be her favorite design for a ship.

For those who wanted bigger and bigger mega-ships, Joan was all for them and understood why so many passengers and cruise lines were drawn to them.

For her however, much like Christian in this regard, her taste ran a bit more toward old-fashioned and sentimental.

For Joan, the Vista Class ships evoked images of the great cruise ships of the 1950s. As Christian mentioned, a much more elegant and simple time.

At full capacity, the Vista ships only held about 2,000 passengers. A number which was being dwarfed by the Mega-ships of today which held almost 7,000 passengers and 3,000 crew members.

Joan still had trouble accepting that a Vista Class ship was now considered midsized or even small by some in the industry. At approximately 90,000 tons, 950 feet in length, 106 feet wide, and with 11 passenger decks, she saw nothing "midsized" or "small" about them.

Rather, she did see them as perfect. And much *more* than perfect to morph into *SW1* and house at least a few hundred Elves, with room for more as the ship's design had about one-thousand passenger cabins.

As she thought all of that, Joan was sitting at one end of the conference table in Christian's office suite next to Jeff Foster, the CEO of the construction company Christian owned, along with one of his top architects. Together, they were pouring over the blueprints for the Vista Class ship Christian just bought.

Christian and Joan had discussed his ideas for the ship and how best to transform it into *SW1* in minute detail on the flight back to Massachusetts from Washington, DC. As Christian excitedly spoke about his plans for *SW1*, Joan really could see the little boy coming out in him. A spirit and an energy which she now knew had been suppressed for decades.

Joan and Christian saw eye-to-eye on the vast majority of his ideas for the ship and *SW1*. As she explained the inner-workings of the Vista Class ship and how it was structured, he changed a few things here and there. But ultimately, they were both in agreement because ultimately, *SW1* was going to become a very small, very secret, and incredibly secluded small town at the very top of the planet earth in its new home at The North Pole.

Because it was going to become a functioning small town, many of the designs already incorporated into the Vista Class ship would remain. The one thousand cabins, the shops, the movie theater, the main restaurant, the coffee shops, the medical center, the chapel, the spa for exercise and relaxation, an expanded library, and the twelve-hundred seat main auditorium at the front of the ship.

What would *not* remain the same would be the crew deck on deck one. While one-third *would* be kept for "crew" cabins, a lounge, and a crew restaurant, two-thirds of it was going to be *transformed* into the workshop where the toys for children would be built by the Elves of *SW1*.

"Elves" who, during the course of their year-long contract, would be able to rotate jobs within *SW1* if desired. If they tired of making toys, they could try their hand in the gift shops, helping out in the restaurant and coffee shops, working in the spa, the movie theater, or the library.

Because of her past experience with Carnival, Joan had learned that the crew of a ship had to stay busy, entertained as much as possible, and not become bored.

Christian agreed with her on that, but only up to a point. As he had explained to her on the flight back to Massachusetts, "The Elves we are seeking are going to be so very different from not only the average crewmember on a cruise ship, but also, the average American or average citizen from any country. Because of who we are looking for and who we will select, our Elves, for the most part, will be faith-filled people looking to make a real and positive difference in life. Most will also believe in the true meaning of Christmas and believe that Christ and the Baby Jesus have to be the integral component to a holiday that honors His birth and bears His name. As mentioned, if some of our Elves are not spiritual but are simply incredibly decent people looking to dedicate one full year of their lives to helping poor and disadvantaged children, they will be warmly welcomed and accepted. But, as our very unique ad is only appearing in faith-based sites and publications, I suspect most of our Elves will believe in the true meaning of Christmas and will want to honor that meaning in a real and lasting way. Because of that, we will select some of the most unselfish and self-sufficient people ever. They will become Elves because they truly want to do good with their lives. And because of who they are, they will be very happy with anything provided for them on the ship in terms of extras or luxuries."

Joan fully agreed with Christian regarding the make-up and quality of people who would become the "Elves" of *SW1*. That said, she still was going to err on the side of having as many extras as possible if for no other reason than as a nice way to say "thank you" for their time, commitment, and sacrifice. She had already decided one of those extras would be a film library of one thousand wholesome movies of almost every genre that could be played on-demand anytime on the 40-inch flat-screen televisions that would be in every cabin onboard *SW1*.

***

At the other end of the conference table, Christian was sitting with his legal counsel Gerry Donovan, Marty Williams, the former Special Forces and CIA operative who was now head of security, and Nina Sobhan.

Suddenly, as Joan, Jeff, and the architect were discussing the options to convert the one thousand-seat entertainment theater into the workshop for *SW1*, they heard Christian raise his voice from the other end of the room.

"Look, Gerry. You and I have been friends for a very long time. You happen to be my friend who *happens* to be my lead lawyer and counsel. Trust me, I really do know that you have my best interests at heart. I really do. But guess what, at the end of the day, it's *my* money and I am going to do what I think best. No offence, but I really don't care if you or anyone else thinks this idea is crazy. I really don't. Your only job with regard to this project is to make sure every single legal angle is covered and that we are protected. That's it..."

Christian stopped when he realized that now everyone in the room was focused on him.

Fine, he thought. They can all hear this again...and for the last time.

"Okay," started Christian again. "Everyone, please listen because I really am only going to say this one more time. I am doing this because it makes me happy. Me. As 'silly,' 'expensive,' 'ridiculous,' or as 'crazy' as the idea of creating *SW1* and locating it at the North Pole might sound to some, it's something I *am* going to do. And on a planet of billions of people, I am hoping and now praying that I will eventually find at least one thousand or so people who share and believe in my 'crazy' vision. Sadly, the fact is that the world is getting more uncertain, more tragic, and more dangerous by the day. There *are* bad people roaming the earth. There *is* true evil out there. This is not the reason for *SW1*, but as a byproduct of where it is going to be located, how nice to know that we can at least create a microcosm of decency, civility, goodwill, and even faith, isolated from man's inhumanity to man. All the while bringing at least flashes of happiness to innocent children who, through no fault of their own, find themselves condemned to lives we would not wish upon our worst enemies."

Christian then took a long drink of water before continuing as he could feel his entire body warming because of the feelings and emotions he was now articulating.

"Look, before my brother showed me the light and saved me, I was on the verge of ending my 'misery.' A misery I had only brought upon myself because of a life led dedicated only to *my* selfish pleasures. Not only did my brother Paul save me, but my vision of *SW1* saved me. It truly did. So no matter if Gerry, if any of you, or if anyone else in the world thinks the idea stupid or crazy, it does not matter. I am doing it with you or without you. Period."

With that, Christian turned and walked out the door of the conference room.

After several seconds, Gerry Donovan spoke up.

"I don't know what I said that was wrong. Christian is my friend and I do support him. I didn't say the project was crazy. Not at all. I was only asking if he was *really* sure about everything because there were going to be a number of legal and financial hoops to jump through to make this all a reality. That's all I said."

"It's alright, brother," said Marty Williams, who tended to call male friends *brother*. "It really is. He knows you've got his back. He really does. He's just got an awful lot on his plate right now and knowing the boss-man, I bet he has not slept more than two hours per night for the last number of days."

Williams had been with Christian for the last six years as the head of his security. Before that, he had spent his government career on the front end of a spear around the world defending his nation. He had seen enough bad things to last several lifetimes and was not only grateful to be working for Christian, but grateful that the two had become close friends over the last few years. No matter what Christian's past personal life had been, he had always treated Marty and his team with the deepest respect and gratitude for their service to our country. Because of that, Marty and his six-man team of experts would follow Christian to the North Pole or anyplace else if necessary.

Gerry Donovan let out a long breath.

"Thanks for saying that, Marty. I hope you're right."

As Gerry finished the sentence, Joan walked to the front of the room.

"If you all will excuse me for a few moments. I'll go and talk to him."

After Joan walked out, Nina turned to face those left in the room.

"I don't know if Christian knows it yet, but she might the best thing that ever happened to him."

CHAPTER NINETEEN

When Joan got to Christian's office door, it was closed.

She softly knocked on it with no response. Knocked again with no response, then slowly opened the door.

She saw that Christian was sitting at his desk with his black, high-back office chair now swiveled so it faced away from her.

As she stepped into the office, she quietly closed the door behind her and then walked the ten steps between her and Christian sitting in his chair.

"Christian," she said in a semi-whisper as she stood to the side of his chair. "Christian. Are you all right?"

When he still did not answer her, she bent down, put her hands on the back of his chair and slowly turned it until he was facing her. When she looked down at him, his eyes were closed, but she could tell that he had been crying.

"Christian," she said as she kneeled on the floor before him. "What is wrong?"

No response.

Joan reached over and held his left hand in her right.

"Christian."

Christian let out a slow breath but kept his eyes closed as he finally answered.

"I'm not really sure. I'm not sure where that emotion came from. Gerry's my friend. I know he's only looking out for me. But no matter what any of you say, I know deep down, all of you have to think this idea is nuts."

Joan let go of his hand and grabbed both arm rests and shook the chair.

"Open your eyes and look at me Christian Nicholas. Open them right now."

Christian did so and was greeted with the sight of Joan kneeling before him with nothing but deep concern flowing from her dark brown eyes. As he looked down at her, he felt she was the most beautiful person from the inside-out that he had ever met in his life. A realization that made him feel all the more uncertain and even confused.

With his eyes now open, Joan leaned over and held both of his hands.

"Listen to me, Christian. *No one* thinks this idea is 'nuts.' No one. Not one of us. All of us think the opposite, in fact. Where is all of this coming from? This is not the military. No one drafted us. And when we have all of the 'Elves' picked out, they will be involved because *they* want to be involved. All those people involved in this project have known you for years and most have been friends with you for years. They are doing this because they want to help you. They are doing this because it actually means something to *them*. In a world being turned more upside down by the day, they are really and truly proud to be involved in this project. And while I have only known you for the last few weeks, I believe in you and I believe in your North Pole Project more than I have ever believed in anything in my life."

"But why?" He asked through watery eyes.

She inched closer to him on the floor as she looked up at him.

"Well, let's just say I'm feeling a bit more protective of you."

He allowed himself a small smile.

"You are?"

She slowly nodded her head. "I am."

He looked down at her now smiling face and—for reasons he still did not yet quite understand—knew she meant it. And because he did believe that, he did suddenly feel calmer and indeed…more protected.

It was truly counter to the experiences he had in the past. Including with his ex-wife. Women who were looking to *take* as much as possible from him with *zero* thoughts of his well-being or protection.

But, as he had already and finally admitted to himself, he picked those women for all the wrong reasons. So, in that sense, he knew the fault was with him.

But now, with Joan, it was different and it was growing from a simple and wonderfully innocent schoolboy crush to something more. Something maybe real.

"Well," he said as he stood and reached out his arm made powerful from daily workouts to lift her from the floor. "The truth is, you are having a very positive effect upon me. And while it's something I've honestly never felt in my life before, I'd very much like to see where our new friendship takes us."

"Me, too," replied Joan who stepped in to hug him.

For several seconds, they remained in that embrace with Joan's head most comfortably resting on Christian's strong chest.

Finally, Christian stepped back and looked down at Joan.

"Thank you...thank you for being you. For being the person you are."

"You are most welcome."

Christian then looked toward the door to his office.

"Okay. Well, I better go find Gerry and apologize. He *is*, after all, my lawyer. As you and I are in here, he might be moping around somewhere and writing me out of my own company," said Christian with a laugh.

CHAPTER TWENTY

Dimitri Kharlamov locked the front door of his small café on the outskirts of Moscow, and started his fifteen-minute solitary walk back to his one-bedroom apartment located in a grey ten-story building that was one of twenty such buildings built back in the day when Russia was part of what was then called the *Soviet Union*.

Dimitri first started to work in the café when it was the "family" café, and he was but a boy of fourteen.

His mother used to tease him all the time that when he was ready, he would be able to pick "any girl in Moscow to be your future wife as they all seem to have a crush on you now."

And indeed, they did.

Dimitri was the busboy for the family café, and all the teen girls, and even a few of the older women, used to make a fuss over him, and tell him how handsome and special he was.

Dimitri was often the cause of arguments between his mother and his father. Because he was an only child and the absolute light of her life, his mother was always spoiling and overprotecting him whereas his father, who'd served in the Russian Army and once played for the famous Moscow Dynamo hockey team, felt his son was being babied by his wife. *He*, as the boy's father, needed to put a stop to it before it was too late.

For the next twenty-six years, Dimitri continued to work in the café. He went from busboy, to cook, to waiter, to part owner. All the while, his "gorgeous" blond hair got progressively thinner and his flat stomach got progressively rounder.

He dated off and on through his secondary years, and even had a girlfriend for a couple of months. But after that, the dates came fewer and further between until they stopped altogether.

Dimitri knew that, unlike his father, he did not look like an athlete or anything close to a male model. But now in his forties, he also knew that in this day and age, more men looked like him rather than some athlete or some unattainable movie star.

He had always assumed he was going to get married one day and have children. More than assumed, he loved the idea and could not wait to begin that phase of his life. A phase that he felt was the natural progression of order.

When he turned forty, his parents gave him the café as a birthday present and announced they were leaving Moscow to live in a condo on a beach on the Black Sea.

Even after they did that and left, Dimitri was still sure there was a woman out there for him; it was only a matter of time. He had friends. He socialized. He had great relationships with the regular customers. People were looking out for him.

All the pieces were in place for him to finally meet a woman who would love him for him. And yet…it did not happen. Ever. Weeks became months and months became a few years.

While at the café, or when bowling or socializing with his friends, Dimitri was always all smiles and personality. He worked hard at fooling people as he did not want anyone to feel sorry for him.

But for the last year especially, when he once again walked into his very neat but always empty one-bedroom apartment, his loneliness all but consumed him.

Of late, he truly felt like he was losing his mind.

Almost every day after work was like going through the grieving process. The sounds of silence and the reality of his loneliness were becoming terrifying to him. Terrifying.

The thought—the realization—that he might *never* find anyone ever and might leave this world alone and unloved by a spouse was becoming all-consuming and too much to bear.

In his desperate search to find out what was happening to his mind, Dimitri had read that a growing number of doctors and psychologists firmly believed that loneliness was the *number one destroyer* of human spirit and hope on the planet. Number one. That it was ultimately responsible for more human pain, suffering, and even loss of human life than almost any disease out there.

As he sat on his sofa and sobbed, he knew that to be the case. For while he had trained himself to put on a brave face to the rest of the world, when he was back behind the closed door of his apartment, the black curtain of loneliness now always closed around him.

"I don't understand," he cried to himself. "I don't understand. I'm a good man. I work hard. I treat people well. I live by the golden rule. I go to church. In a world of billions of people, is there no one for me? No one. *No one*. Why? I don't understand. I don't understand…"

As he continued to cry, he knew he was far from alone in the world. His readings had also informed him that in each and every country on earth, there were countless people just like him. Countless.

Very good, very kind, and very decent men and women who had never found the soulmate they had been seeking. Very good, very kind, and very decent men and women who had to come to grips with the awful fact that they might very well spend the rest of their lives…alone.

Dimitri knew that loneliness did destroy the human mind. That it did destroy hope. That it *was* a killer.

He knew all of that but knew something even worse.

He knew he was losing the strength to fight it very much longer. He knew he was losing the battle.

Unless someone experienced such constant and unrelenting loneliness, then they could never understand its totally destructive effects. Ever.

After his sobbing finally stopped and the tears came no more for now, Dimitri slowly stood, walked into his bathroom, and washed his face with warm water.

Then, after he ate dinner all alone once again at his small table in his small kitchen, he walked into his bedroom to check his computer. It, like the television in the living room, were the last defenses against the ravages of loneliness.

They at least provided some company for his damaged mind. But even those welcome and needed distractions were being ground down to rubble by the ever-marching darkness of loneliness. He was painfully aware he would soon have no tools left to fight off his constant enemy.

That day, he knew, was soon approaching and what truly scared him, in a small but growing part of his mind, was that he was looking forward to that moment. A moment that part of his mind was trying to convince him would represent lasting freedom from the unimaginable pain of loneliness.

Dimitri shook his head to clear it as he typed in the IP address for his local church. Because he was both a man of faith and it was a way to be among people, he had volunteered at the church for the last ten years.

After scanning the home page, he quickly looked at that week's schedule. Then, he clicked on the ad page for that week.

His mother and a growing number of his friends had counseled him to get a pet. He really didn't have the mental energy to care for a cat or a dog, but nonetheless, he took a quick look just to satisfy his own curiosity.

As that page popped-up on his screen, his eyes were immediately drawn to a small ad placed at the very bottom right-hand side.

He read the ad and then he read it again.

He stood up, walked to his refrigerator, grabbed a bottle of Coke, then sat back down in front of his computer and read the ad again.

For some reason, as mysterious as the small ad was, it was speaking to him in a very large way. The more Dimitri read it, the more excited he became.

So few words written in such a mysterious way and yet…they unexplainably sparked a light within him. A light that had not been there for years.

"What do I have to lose?" He asked himself with a sudden smile happily appearing on his face. "What do I have to lose?"

CHAPTER TWENTY-ONE

One week later, Christian, Joan, Nina Sobhan, Jeff Foster, and two architects from Jeff's construction company were seated in Christian's Gulfstream G650 private jet as it made its way from Massachusetts to Italy.

They were on their way to Trieste, Italy, to meet some of the senior executives and architects of Fincantieri, the world's premier shipbuilding company.

For the last two hours, as the Gulfstream G650 easily powered its way across the Atlantic Ocean at a cruising altitude of 40,000 feet, Christian had been pouring over the annual reports, press releases, and media stories related to Fincantieri.

"This company is amazing," Christian said out loud as much to himself as the others on the aircraft. "Really incredible."

"Yes, Christian," answered Joan from the front of the very large and very luxurious private jet where she was sitting at a table with Jeff Foster making sure the blueprints were ready to be reviewed by the architects from Fincantieri. "I've been telling you that for weeks now."

"I know," said Christian with a smile as he stuck his head out into the aisle to get a better look at Joan twenty feet in front of him. "But have you *read* all of this background on these guys?"

"No," answered Joan with a growing smile. "I didn't have to. I have sailed on a number of their ships and know they are the best. That is why I am so happy *SW1* will be one of their ships."

"Yeah," said Christian once again sounded like an excited little boy, a state of being that made Joan quite happy. "That's great that you sailed on their ships and all of that. Great. But listen to this. Fincantieri, in one form or another, has been around for over 230 years. Are you *kidding* me? They have basically been building ships for as long as the United States of America has existed. Amazing. They have over 20,000 employees in Italy, the rest of Europe, the Americas, and Asia working in over twenty shipyards they own. They basically build ships for *everyone*. They build cruise ships, merchant ships, and naval vessels. Every major cruise line interested in a meaningful history of real-world experience combined with the highest of quality, goes back to them time and time again for their ships."

"Yes, Christian," said Joan again with a smile as she turned her head back to look down at the blueprints before her.

"Nina," said Christian as he leaned over the aisle and touched her on the arm without looking at her.

Each of the eight first-class seats plus two sofas on the Gulfstream G650 could be converted into flat beds and while Nina hadn't done that, she had her seat reclined about forty-five degrees with her eyes closed as she tried to catch up on some sleep.

"Hmmm…what?" answered Nina as she stirred from her sleep.

Christian now looked over at her and his eyes widened.

"Whoops. So sorry. I didn't realize you were trying to rest."

Nina blinked her eyes a few times at first, looked out the oval window next to her, then turned her head to the right to look at her boss.

"I wasn't trying to *rest*, Christian. I was *sound* asleep."

"Oh," said Christian as he giggled. "I said I was sorry."

Aside from his most loyal employee at his firm, over the years, Nina had become like the little sister he never had. Not only did he confide in her about a number of private matters, but developed a warm, almost sibling rivalry, which saw them playfully bickering from time to time.

"It's not funny, Christian," said Nina as she rubbed her eyes.

"Okay," said Christian as he giggled again. "To show you how sorry I am, I will give you permission to go up to the galley and get yourself an extra cookie. But only one. Happy now?"

Nina laughed out loud.

"You are *such* a goofball. How in the world did *you* become a billionaire?"

"First," said Christian as he pretended to look serious. "I'm a *multi*billionaire. Second, that's a question I ask myself every day."

Nina simply shook her head.

"So…you wanted something from me?"

"Well, since you're awake *anyway*…"

Since he was a little boy, Christian could often not help himself when it came to sneaking in just one more "in-your-face" remark. Once when he was eight and his brother Paul was ten, the two of them kept laughing and making noise well after bedtime. Their Army sergeant dad had come into the bedroom twice to tell them to "knock it off and go to sleep." The second time, their dad added, "If I hear just *one more peep* from this room, someone is getting a spanking."

Just as his dad was closing their bedroom door, little Christian waited, and waited, and waited, and when the door was just an inch from being all the way closed, he said, "Peep."

To this day, his brother still kids him about the spanking he got that night.

Nina couldn't help but laugh when she looked at his now, truly childlike face.

"Okay, okay. Enough. What do you need?"

"Fincantieri. Who are we meeting from there again?"

Nina reached down into the briefcase on the floor next to her and pulled out her tablet.

After a few strokes, she looked over at Christian.

"Well, thanks to *Joan* and *her* connections," she emphasized, loud enough for Randall to hear up front, "you are actually having a late dinner tonight with the Chairman and the CEO."

"Wow. Awesome," said Christian as he went back to his reading material.

CHAPTER TWENTY-TWO

Carol MacKenzie stood in the living room of her small two-bedroom apartment in Edmonton, Alberta, Canada, and tried to remember.

As she moved some of her snow white hair away from her face, she continually blinked her still bright blue eyes as she fought to think.

She knew she was standing up because she was about to head out the door to drive down to the local store to pick up a few things for their home, but now, she could not remember where she left the keys to her car.

Carol quickly looked over at her sister Dottie sitting on the sofa as she read that morning's newspaper.

Dottie, at seventy-eight, was the older sister of Carol by four years. She felt her younger sister's eyes now upon her, but had trained herself not to look up or react to these episodes of Carol's newfound "forgetfulness."

Ever so slowly, Dottie had been morphing from older sister to caregiver and protector. Five years earlier, after Dottie had lost her husband of forty-nine years, Carol insisted that she move in with her.

Carol had been always very comfortable on her own and decided at a very early age, that she was going to be, as she laughingly joked, "a confirmed bachelorette."

And she had. Carol never married, she'd worked for the same company in Edmonton for thirty years, attended the same church, retired, and found great comfort and companionship with her faith and the greater "MacKenzie Clan" in and around Edmonton.

But of late, Carol also knew something was wrong. Something that was confirmed to her by her doctor two months earlier. That being that she was in the, as he put it, "early stages of Alzheimer's disease."

Doctor "John," who had been a family friend for over forty years, confided in her that "you have a year, maybe two of relatively good time before you will need supervised care."

"Two years," Carol had been silently repeating in her mind over and over again for the last two months. "Two years."

That very night right before going to bed and right after her prayers, she made a promise to herself. "I am not going to ever feel sorry for myself. Ever. I am going to be of joy, make every second count, and find a way to pass my joy along to others."

Now, standing in the living room not remembering where she left her car keys was an ironic reminder that her mind was fighting against a very real and very scary schedule. A schedule that Carol hoped and prayed could be stretched out a bit longer than predicted.

Carol then shook her head and walked into her bedroom to search for her missing car keys.

As soon as she did, Dottie got up from the sofa, walked into the kitchen, opened the refrigerator, saw the car keys sitting next to the bottle of orange juice, and quickly scooped them up, closed the refrigerator door and walked as quietly as she could back to the living room where she placed the keys back where Carol normally left them.

No sooner had Dottie sat back down than Carol walked out of her bedroom empty handed and looking more than a little frustrated.

"What seems to be the problem, dear?" asked Dottie.

Carol, deep in thought, did not answer right away.

"Carol," began Dottie again. "What is wrong?"

"Oh," answered Carol as offered up a smile to try and mask her worry. "I can't seem to find my car keys."

Dottie smiled with all the love she had in her heart for her younger sister.

"Aren't they sitting right there on the bookcase where you always leave them?"

Carol looked over and darned if they weren't right there. Even though she was happy to see them, she knew something was not quite adding up.

As she walked over to grab the keys, Dottie spoke to her again while patting the sofa cushion next to her.

"Carol, before you go, please sit with me for a minute. I want to show you something I picked up at Mass on Sunday."

Carol looked over and saw Dottie take a little flyer out of the magazine she had been reading. A flyer from their local church.

"What is it?" asked Carol as she sat next to her sister.

"Well," answered Dottie as she put her reading glasses on. "I'm not exactly sure. But it's the most intriguing little help wanted ad I have ever read."

CHAPTER TWENTY-THREE

At 11:00 PM that night Italian time, Christian and Joan were having coffee and dessert with the chairman and CEO of Fincantieri in a private dining room at their corporate headquarters in Trieste, Italy.

"Remarkable," said the Chairman. "Simply remarkable."

"Thank you, Roberto," answered Christian. "I can't tell you how touched I am to hear you say that."

Thanks entirely to Joan and her connections, they did get the dinner with the top leadership of Fincantieri. And for the last ninety minutes or so, Christian and Joan—but mostly Christian—had been explaining the vision for *SW1* and its mission to help poor and disadvantaged children the world over.

"Christian, Joan," began the CEO and the man tasked with the day-to-day running of Fincantieri. "We have the honor of helping a great many deserving charities, both here in Italy and around the world. But I think I can speak for myself and Roberto when I say that this…this vision of yours, has truly and deeply touched us all."

"Thank you, Marco," answered Joan and Christian at the same time.

"You are most welcome. Now, with your permission, I am going to speak with Roberto in Italian for just a few seconds."

As the two very distinguished looking men spoke to each other in Italian, Joan and Christian exchanged a quick look of curiosity.

Suddenly, both men stood up.

"Joan, Christian," said the chairman now as he looked down at the couple. "Would you mind if we stepped out of the room for just a few minutes. We need to check on a couple of issues."

"Of course not," said Christian. "Take as much time as you need."

Marco then leaned down and patted him on the back.

"It will be but a few minutes. In the meantime," he said as he waved over one of the two incredibly professional waiters standing off to the side but always ready, "have some more of our great Italian espresso and tiramisu. We will be right back."

***

About fifteen minutes later, the two men returned to the executive dining room of Fincantieri.

Oddly, to Christian and Joan, when they sat back down, both men also seemed to be sharing the same somber expression.

"Christian," began Marco, "unfortunately, we just discovered that there is a serious problem with regard to the sale of this ship to you."

"Pardon me," asked Christian as he was instantly trying to go over the finances and details of the transaction in his mind.

"*Very* serious," added the chairman of the company.

Christian looked over at Joan who now looked as confused and concerned as him.

"I don't think I understand," said Christian.

"Well," continued Marco, "we just spoke with the head of our accounting department and it appears we will no longer be able to sell you the ship at the agreed upon price."

Christian sat bolt upright in his chair.

"What? Wait a minute. We have a deal. The papers have been signed."

"That is right," answered Marco. "We do have a contract. But it is a bad one. One that we will no longer honor."

"Just a second, Marco," said Joan suddenly getting a very sick feeling in her stomach as she was the one who'd recommended this company in the first place. "I agree with Christian. A deal has been signed. Marco, I have known you and Roberto for many years and…"

Marco held up his right hand.

"Yes. A deal was signed. But mistakes of course do happen from time to time. Even in a very careful and detailed oriented company like ours. But...there *has* been a mistake. Because of that mistake, we will no longer honor the contract signed. The reason being that upon further review of *that* contract, it appears we somehow *overcharged* you for the ship. You should be getting that ship at *cost* to us. So...our most sincere apologies for that error on our part."

Joan involuntarily brought her right hand up to her mouth. "At cost" to Fincantieri meant that Christian would be saving tens of millions of dollars. Millions he could pour back into the project.

"To make up for this inadvertent mistake," added the Chairman with a twinkle now in his eyes, "Fincantieri would also like to make a generous donation to *SW1* every year of its existence."

Christian caught his breath as he looked at the now smiling faces of the two men sitting across from him. As he did, he became overwhelmed and stood up from the table and walked over to the windows out of embarrassment.

Ten seconds later, a strong arm draped itself across his shoulders.

Christian turned his face, and through watery eyes, saw the smiling and clearly proud face of the CEO of Fincantieri.

"Christian," said Marco, "there is no need to hide your emotions or your tears. What we are doing now is the least we can do. You have inspired us with this vision of yours. We are deeply honored that one of *our* ships will be the home of *SW1*. We are humbled to know that through your generosity, ultimately millions of poor and deserving children will be touched in such a positive and meaningful way. Trust me, Christian. It is us and our company, who want to thank *you* for letting us be a part of something that really will make a difference."

Christian took a deep breath and wiped his eyes with the napkin he still held in his hand.

He then turned, looked at the CEO, gave him a hug, and stood back.

"Thank you, Marco. Thank you. And, sorry. I *have* been very emotional of late. But what you are doing is so special. It's so easy to lose faith in humanity and then when someone does something so amazing, so generous..."

"You are most welcome. Most welcome." Then with a broad smile, the CEO added, "Most of us lose faith at some point. In humanity, in religion, and even in ourselves. No? But then, if we are lucky and blessed, we are touched by something which reinforces our faith. Makes us stronger. Unites us. You touched us in such a way tonight."

Christian took another deep breath and then nodded his head.

"So," finished Marco as his smile grew larger. "Tomorrow, we will take you to our shipyard in Monfalcone to see your ship. To see, what *will* become your *SW1*."

***

At 10:00 the next morning, Christian, Joan, Nina, and Jeff Foster were picked up in front of their hotel by a van from Fincantieri for the thirty-minute ride from Trieste to the Monfalcone shipyard.

As Christian sat next to Joan right behind the driver as the luxury van made its way toward the shipyard, he kept fidgeting in his seat.

Joan looked over at him to make sure he was all right and saw that his eyes were bright and wide open taking in the scenery. He had a huge smile plastered across his handsome face.

"What are you thinking?" she asked.

"Well," he said as he turned to aim his smile at her. "Ironically and quite appropriately, I am thinking about Christmas."

"In what way?"

"Now," he said as his smile grew even wider. "Right this second as we are on the way to the shipyard, I feel like a child walking down the stairs on Christmas Day getting ready to unwrap my dream present sitting under the Christmas tree."

"I know what you mean. This is actually very exciting. In the history of the world, no one has ever done anything like this, and now—thanks to you—we are about to get our first look at what is going to become an actual toy factory at the North Pole. A fantasy, a myth, and a dream is about to become a reality. It's all still very surreal to me."

"Well," said Christian as he placed his right arm behind her on the seat. "What we are about to see in a few minutes is thanks to *you* and *your* incredible connections. As for it being surreal, it is indeed. But every single day I am more and more convinced that I—and now, we—are doing what we are *supposed* to be doing. I feel it. I really do."

Joan nodded in agreement as Christian turned his head to look back out the window in his growing excitement.

CHAPTER TWENTY-FOUR

For the next twenty minutes, Joan was beyond content to sit next to Christian and simply think. Think about him and think about her.

In her mind, meeting the man he had become was as surreal as the project she had just embarked upon.

At least to herself, she could admit that she *was* an intelligent and accomplished woman. She understood that she was very attractive and a "real catch" as her sister Janice and a few of her really close friends always told her.

She had been on a number of first dates in her life. Almost all of which stayed "first dates."

Then, as she became more successful and well-known in the business community, a series of CEOs, millionaires, and celebrities showed their interest. Even a couple of billionaires in the Miami area.

But Joan also understood that to them, she was just a "trophy." She did understand that at least in a physical sense, she was very attractive to these men because of her looks, her figure, and her position in the business community.

But, because of the constant prodding of her sister and her truly close friends, she did, against her better judgment, go on a few first dates with these very wealthy and "accomplished" men. Only to have her judgment confirmed.

After a series of first date disappointments, Joan began to wonder if there were something wrong with *her*? Could the truth be that for some reason she was incapable of feeling love? Incapable of falling in love?

And then...and then...when she had very comfortably resigned herself to the fact that she might never meet that special someone...*he* called out of the blue.

A man who, as her memory instantly reminded her, was *worse* than the rich "one-date-wonders" she had gone out with. A person who, while quite possibly being the most handsome man she had ever met in her life, came across as only "in love" with his mirror and who *did* view women in the most basic and condescending of ways.

But then this "poster boy" for all that was wrong with men apologized to her on the phone, stripped away his superficial coverings, and laid himself and his emotions bare.

And for the first time in her life...something clicked deep within her. Just a glimmer of something, but something for sure.

And then she was reintroduced to the new Christian Nicholas. Not the arrogant and condescending man she had met in the green-room of CNBC years earlier, but someone who *had* just stood on the edge of oblivion, who *did* have a real and miraculous epiphany, and who had come through the experience to become the man he now was. The man he was meant to be.

And out of nowhere, she developed real feelings for him. And he with her.

"There she is."

The words of the driver snapped Joan out of her very pleasant thoughts.

The words of the driver also caused Christian to almost jump out of his seat with pure excitement and joy.

"Oh, my gosh," yelled Christian. "Oh, my gosh. Joan! Can you see it? Holy cow."

Joan leaned across Christian to get a better look at a class of ship she had seen so many times before.

But when she saw it, she was hit with a wave of excitement she had never felt before. She was *not* looking at a class of ship she had seen before, but rather, at a magical and wondrous *dream* that was becoming a reality. A dream that was going to touch innocent and needy children the world over.

"Yes, Christian. I see it. I really and truly do see it."

When the van pulled to a stop and they all got off, they were greeted by the smiling faces of Roberto and Marco.

After hugs and kisses were exchanged, Marco put his arm once again around Christian's shoulders as he pointed to the ship.

"So…what do you think of the ship? The soon-to-be-historic home of *SW1*?"

Christian looked up and up and up. He was in total agreement with Joan. It was simply beyond him how a ship basically fifteen stories tall, over three football fields long, and 90,000 tons could be considered "mid-sized" or even "small" by today's ship standards. It looked absolutely massive to him.

"It's simply the most incredible structure I have ever seen in my life. I can't believe it's real."

"Oh, but it is, Christian. Today you will touch her, walk on her, and see your very vision coming to life."

"I don't know how to thank you."

"Christian, please," said the CEO. "We had already built her for someone else. She is ninety percent done. You know that."

"And I will say '*please*' to you as well, Marco. The generosity and kindness you and Roberto showed us last night is beyond my ability to comprehend. I am still stunned by this gesture. I will treasure it always."

"Thank you," answered Marco. "As we will treasure our new friendship with all of you."

The CEO then directed Christian closer to the rest of the group. As he did, Joan stepped forward.

She was wearing snow white Prada pants and a matching jacket. Under the jacket was a hot pink blouse with her feet sporting three-inch-tall, hot pink stilettos.

"Joan," said Roberto with a smile. "As I mentioned to you last time you were here on business for Carnival—while you are, or *were,* the best and most accomplished CEO in the industry…*by far*—you also deserve to be on the movie screen or in the pages of the best fashion magazines."

"Thank you, Roberto," answered Joan.

"And Joan and Christian," the Chairman quickly continued. "I hope that is all right to say. My apologies if not, but here in Italy, we still like to celebrate and acknowledge true beauty. In whatever form, it might take."

"I could not agree more, Roberto," answered Christian with a warm laugh. "The world is becoming much too sensitive. Soon, we won't even be able to look someone square in the eyes out of fear of offending them."

"Well, thank you all," said Joan as she switched to her executive voice and turned to look at the chairman of Fincantieri. "Now, if it's all right with you and Marco, Jeff Foster and his team will stay behind to work with your architects to make the final modifications to the ship."

"But of course," nodded the chairman. "We would be honored to host them."

"Excellent," said Christian as he clapped his hands together. He then looked back up at the ship. "Wow."

"Speaking of those modifications," continued the chairman. "Please don't be put off by the color of the ship now. That is simply gray primer. When you figure out what colors..."

"Oh, but I have," interjected Christian as he stepped closer to the ship and looked up.

The two executives from Fincantieri looked at each other, and then at Joan and Jeff. All four were now smiling as they were caught up in the childlike enthusiasm of Christian.

"You, have?" said Marco with a chuckle. "And what might those be?"

Christian turned back to face the group.

"The hull of the ship is going to be kelly green. The funnel is going to be candy red, and...sorry...Joan...what's the name of that big 'light-bulb' looking protrusion at the front of the cruise ships?"

Joan could not help herself and began to laugh.

"It's called the bulbous bow."

"Yes. Exactly," confirmed Marco. "The bulbous bow is now essential to basically every ship on the ocean. It is incredibly efficient at not only redirecting the tremendous forces of hydrodynamic resistance and drag, but it really does make for a smoother and faster journey."

While Christian may have been grateful for the textbook explanation, it was clear that his mind was still focused on more basic thoughts.

"Yeah," reinforced Christian. "That thing. The bulbous bow. That has to be painted neon red. Neon."

"Neon," repeated the CEO of Fincantieri. "That's very specific. Why?"

"For Rudolph's nose," answered Christian with a very straight face.

Both Joan and Jeff Foster almost doubled-over in laughter from his answer.

The two leaders of Fincantieri exchanged looks of confusion.

"Rudolph?" said the Chairman. "I don't think we..."

"You know," continued Christian with his still straight face. "Rudolph. From '*Rudolph the Red-Nosed Reindeer.*'"

"Ah, yes," answered the CEO as he figured out what Christian was talking about. "My children used to watch that. Yes, very funny, Christian. Very funny."

"I don't think he's kidding, Marco," said Joan who softly began to laugh again at the surreal wonder of it all. "Are you, Christian?"

"No." answered Christian as a smile now appeared on his face. "I'm actually not. It has to be *neon red.*"

The CEO looked toward the front of the ship, nodded his head, and then turned to face Christian.

"Then neon red it shall be, in honor of Rudolph."

***

For the next four-plus hours, the group toured every inch of the ship.

Christian wanted to walk up and down every deck. See the galley. See the engine room. Walk into all of the public rooms. See the passenger cabins that the "Elves" would soon call home. And then simply sit in the spectacular lobby and take it all in.

Once seated in the lobby and sensing that he wanted to be on his own to digest what he had just taken in, the others stood about one hundred feet off to the side and talked among themselves.

After a few minutes, out of the corner of his eye, Marco noticed that Christian had stood up.

He then slowly walked over to him.

"Christian," began Marco, in a somewhat nervous voice. "Would it be all right if I asked you for a personal favor?"

"Marco," smiled Christian. "After what all of you and the company did last night, you are entitled to endless favors. Please do so."

"Well..." began the CEO as he adjusted the collar of his shirt. "Early this morning over breakfast, I spoke to my mother and father who, thankfully, though they are both in their mid-70s, are in excellent health. More thankfully for me is the fact that they live with my wife and I, and have been the most wonderful grandparents ever. So, when we spoke this morning, I told them of what you are doing. Of how it came to you and how it is your plan to spend the rest of your life helping the most-deserving children in the world.

"I should tell you they are both people of deep faith. They go to Mass every day. When I told them, my mother actually cried in happiness at the joy of it all. After telling them, I went to my bedroom to brush my teeth and get ready to leave. When I came back out, my mother and father were both waiting for me. They had the biggest smiles I had ever seen on their faces. Christian…"

Now, it was Marco's eyes that began to tear-up. As they did, he stopped for just a moment as he took a breath and then looked around the lobby before looking back at Christian.

"Christian…they asked me…they asked me…to ask you…if they could *volunteer* to go with you all. They asked me to ask you if they could be two of your 'Elves' on *SW1*."

"Marco," said Christian in awe as he stepped closer to the CEO. "Did they really ask that? Oh, my goodness. Wow. *Nothing* could make me prouder or more honored. When *SW1* is ready for her journey north and if your parents still want to come, we will all be thrilled to welcome them into the family."

CHAPTER TWENTY-FIVE

James Rawlings III stepped out of his twenty-million-dollar brownstone townhome on Park Avenue—just several blocks down from the Waldorf Astoria—and into the back seat of a brand-new, black Mercedes 500 sedan. Once in, his chauffer Ken quietly closed the door after the impeccably dressed man with his well-known mane of still-thick, snow white hair and quickly assumed his place behind the steering wheel.

"Off to the club as usual, Mr. Rawlings?" asked the chauffer, who had been driving James Rawlings III for the last ten years.

Rawlings did not answer right away. Instead, the sixty-four-year-old retired industrialist simply stared out the window at the townhouse he had paid cash for several years before.

Before his retirement, Rawlings had been the CEO of a Fortune 50 company during which his average compensation had been in the neighborhood of forty-five million dollars per year for the last fifteen years. The prior ten years before that, his compensation had averaged thirty million per year.

Exactly one year ago today, he had retired. And since the very day he had retired, he had been miserable.

But, if he at least admitted the truth to himself—as he had decided to do that very morning as he looked into his reflection in the mirror of his still bright and clear blue eyes while shaving—then he knew he had been miserable at least for several years before retiring.

Worse than miserable, he simply felt empty inside. Rudderless. Nothing.

If he was lucky, he knew he might have twenty more years of QTL— or Quality Time Left—on earth.

"To do what," he silently asked himself as he let out a long sigh. "Pamper ourselves more? Buy more toys for ourselves? Go to more and more high-priced events full of equally superficial people who do not in the least, care about us and are not our friends?"

At that very moment and as he contemplated that question, his wife Jill was attending yet another fashion show for "Charity."

It was about the thirtieth charity fashion show she had attended that year. While she would not admit it, both she, and most assuredly James, knew the main motivation for many of the ultra-wealthy people to attend such shows was *not* to help charity, but rather, to get their names and most especially photos of themselves, in the society sections of the various New York City newspapers, magazines, and television shows.

These never-ending events were put on to feed the insecure and needy egos of New York City's wealthiest and most superficial people. The little money that did actually make its way to a charity was really just an unintended consequence.

As Rawlings sat in the back of his Mercedes and stared mindlessly through the heavily tinted side window of the sedan at the pedestrians passing by, he knew that as much as these events now made his skin crawl, his wife of forty years truly loved and needed them.

When she wasn't attending event after event in the false name of charity, she could be found most nights in the sitting room of their master bedroom on the third floor of their ten-thousand-square-foot home texting or making endless calls to spread gossip, rumors, or criticism of other "friends."

"What have we become?"

"Pardon me, Mr. Rawlings?" asked the chauffer as he caught the eyes of his boss in the rear-view mirror.

Rawlings looked startled for a second.

"Oh…sorry, Ken. I didn't realize I said that out loud."

Ken turned in his seat to face Rawlings.

"You okay, boss?"

During their ten years together, Rawlings had never treated Ken as staff or as an employee, but always as a friend.

While Ken certainly knew and understood he was staff and was an employee—and was always careful to be very respectful of that fact—he also knew that in James Rawlings, he had a genuine friend. Someone who had invited him, his wife, and even their children out to lunch and dinner numerous times over the last decade. And someone who had even come to their home to socialize and most especially that one time when his wife Sarah had double pneumonia and things had been touch and go for a while.

Because of all that and more, Ken had become very protective of his boss over the last few years.

As Ken turned his neck to get a good look at his boss, Rawlings was back to staring out the window.

"Boss..."

Rawlings blinked several times quickly and then turned to look at his friend, who happened to be his very loyal driver.

"I'm sorry, Ken. What?"

"I was just wondering if you were okay," said the driver with a caring smile.

Rawlings looked back out the window at his multimillion-dollar home and then finally, back at Ken.

"No," he answered softly. "No. I guess I'm not all right and I haven't been all right for a long time."

"Is there anything I can do?"

Rawlings turned his head again and spotted a church which was diagonally across from his home sitting on the corner of Park Avenue and 38th Street. He knew that it was called The Church of our Saviour and that it was a well-known landmark in New York City. Other than that, he had never even been inside it in all of these years.

"Actually, there is." Rawlings answered with a smile. "Shut off the engine and walk with me over to that church. I think...I think I need to say a prayer."

CHAPTER TWENTY-SIX

Four weeks later, Christian's entire team—including Ed Rogers flying up from DC—were gathered in the conference room of his headquarters in Westwood, Massachusetts.

"Okay," began Christian who was standing at the head of the table with everyone else seated around it. "First, a few incredibly great updates. Thanks to Joan, we now have the crew and the staff hired for *SW1*. All understand the mission and that is why all signed up. The new captain of *SW1* is a former captain for Cunard and the *QM2* so it doesn't get much better than that. Joan tells me the rest of the officers and crew formerly worked for Carnival Cruise Line, Princess, and Holland America. Again, all signed up first and foremost because they do believe in the true meaning of Christmas and do want to help children in need. Just incredible work by Joan in really, no amount of time…"

Those around the table looked over at Joan and applauded.

Joan nodded her head as she tried not to blush.

"Next," continued Christian, "Ed Rogers gave me some great news last night. All of which is highly confidential and *must* be kept in this room. Thanks to the 'unofficial' and 'it never happened' help from the White House, when she is ready—which will be very soon—*SW1* will sail from Italy to Norfolk, Virginia. She will enter the naval base there in the middle of the night. Then, once all is ready and all of our 'Elves' have been selected, they will all be transported to the base. Once there, they will board *SW1* for a few days of orientation. That will also give any 'Elves' who have a change of heart, time to leave if they so choose.

"Once training is over and everything is in place—which should be late June or early July—a U.S. naval ice breaker will rendezvous with *SW1* in the harbor and, under the darkness of night, lead her out of the harbor and into the open ocean on the way to the North Pole. So…thanks to Ed for all of that great work—also in an impossibly short amount of time."

Everyone around the table looked over at Ed and smiled.

"What?" said Rogers in mock protest. "Joan gets applause and I only get polite smiles."

"People, please," said Christian as he made a motion for everyone to stand. "Join me in a standing ovation for Ed."

Everyone stood up and applauded as they looked over at Ed with smiles.

As they all then sat back now, Christian looked over at Joan. "Don't worry, Joan. Your applause was spontaneous. Some people…have to beg. But we do what we can to please the insecure."

"Oh, yeah," answered Rogers with a laugh. "Let's head out now for 18 holes and when we are done, I'll *own* this place."

"I'd rather walk into a cage of hungry tigers," said Christian before looking over at Nina and smiling. "Oh, and Nina, when this meeting is over, please cut Ed's retainer in half."

Everyone, most of all Rogers, laughed at that.

"Seriously, Ed" said Christian when they were done laughing, "thank you for everything. You are much more than a friend to me, and I couldn't have done any of this without you."

"Thank you, Christian. This whole project simply humbles me and I am very proud to be a part of it."

Christian nodded.

"Next," he went on. "Jeff Foster reported in from Italy to tell me *all* of the modifications to *SW1* have been completed. Santa's workshop now takes up the front two-thirds of all of Deck One. As we speak, it is being stocked with the supplies needed to make the toys for this year.

"Now, as we also discussed, these toys are going to be very retro in nature and relatively easy to build. No electronics, no gadgets. Much more like the toys from—and sorry to bring up this show again, but I love it—The Island of Misfit Toys from *Rudolph the Red-Nosed Reindeer*. The whole idea here, is to simply give children who have less than nothing, a toy of their very own. Something to make them smile. For at least a minute. Something...that will truly be made with all of the love in the world by our Elves."

"Well," said Ed. "Speaking of all of that—meaning the toys and the children—who are the children going to be? There are tens of millions of desperately poor and deserving children around the world. If you hope to pull something off by *this* Christmas, how in the world will you identify some children by then?"

"Perfect timing for that question, Ed," answered Christian. "Also as we speak, my dedicated and highly educated staff of analysts on the second floor of our building is putting the finishing touches on identifying five hundred orphanages around the world."

"Orphanages," repeated Ed as a smile of understanding began to grow on his face.

"Well," continued Christian. "They don't call them 'orphanages' so much anymore. I think in the United States, they are called 'group homes' and the like. Some of the children in these group homes are not true orphans; many were removed from their biological parents because of severe neglect, drugs, or other abuses. Elsewhere around the world, true orphanages still exist.

"As we keep talking about, at the end of the day, we can't even put a Band-Aid on the issues of childhood poverty, dysfunction, and neglect. But we can and will help as many as possible. Again, while everyone will get a toy, some will also get food, medicine, and books. For this first Christmas—which is really a trial run for all of us—we have only picked orphanages and group homes in North America, including Mexico, and the Northern Hemisphere of the world. Purely for logistical reasons. We need to take baby steps before we can walk and eventually...run. My staff tells me that within these five hundred orphanages and group homes are upwards of 100,000 children.

"So, also as we speak, one of the companies I own is testing and perfecting the system we will be using to deliver all of those toys, food, books and medicine to those orphanages and group homes—taking into consideration the different time-zones—*exactly* at midnight on Christmas Eve."

"And how," asked Rogers as he scratched his head, "are you planning to pull off *that* little miracle?"

"Drones," answered Christian with a huge smile.

CHAPTER TWENTY-SEVEN

Ray Thompson slowly drove his twenty-year-old black, rusted-out Ford F-150 pickup truck through the gates of the "Star-Light-Star-Bright" trailer park ten miles outside of Memphis, Tennessee.

Two minutes later, he parked next to a small, equally rusted-out two-bedroom trailer.

He turned off the lights of the truck, shut off the engine, and then rested his head on the steering wheel and began to sob.

He had just put in another sixteen hours as a day laborer. One of the few jobs he could get…because of his record.

Five years earlier, at the age of twenty-eight, he had a good paying job as a forklift operator at one of the big box stores. As he was using the forklift to pick up a pallet of fifty pound bags of mulch, the load suddenly shifted. Before he knew it, he was on the floor with hundreds of pounds of mulch on top of him. Worse than that, the falling mulch had caused the forklift to somehow tip over from the crashing weight.

It was the forklift, the doctors had told him, that broke his back.

One second, he was a six-foot, two-hundred-pound man with a new bride and a promising life in front of him. The next, he was in wheelchair at a VA rehabilitation hospital trying to learn how to walk again.

Slowly, but surely, he *did* learn how to walk again. No one ever questioned his toughness. Not when he'd served his nation overseas in the United States Army, and not now.

But no matter how tough he truly was or how tough others thought he was, it was the pain, the unbearable and constant pain, that was breaking him.

Years earlier as a nineteen-year-old soldier in Afghanistan, he had been wounded in a firefight. The pain of that searing wound paled in comparison to the unrelenting pain that now plagued him morning, noon, and night.

The answer from the doctors at the VA was to simply keep upping the dosage of his already very strong painkiller.

A year after Ray Thompson was out, the doctors decided that he didn't need the painkillers anymore. That he was "most likely exaggerating the pain."

They cut his dose in half, then in half again, and finally stopped it altogether.

Ray Thompson became convinced that he would lose his mind from the pain and withdrawal or do something much worse.

In desperation, he went to a buddy of his from the Army who knew a guy. For one hundred dollars, that guy have him a forged prescription.

While Ray Thompson was waiting at the pharmacy for the prescription to be filled, the pharmacist stepped out of sight to make a phone call. Three minute later, two police officers walked in and arrested Ray on the spot.

Because of his clean record and his service to his country, the judge gave him probation and community service.

Three weeks later, Ray was before the same judge for the same crime.

This time, he got six months in county jail not only for the forged prescription, but because he'd tried to sell half of the pills to an undercover cop for food money.

While in jail, two good things *did* happen. The first was that he was able to stop his addiction to the painkillers. The next was that the pain slowly did start to subside.

Then, once out, a new and morale-breaking reality hit.

Because of his record...because of *his* mistakes...no one would hire him. No one.

The only work he could get was either under the table, or by arriving at the local 7-11 at 5:30 in the morning in the hopes of being picked for a day-labor crew.

Three months after their marriage, Ray and his wife Terri had bought a beautiful three-bedroom, two and one-half bathroom condo.

Both had come from very humble and hardworking families. Together, they could not believe how blessed they were to own such a wonderful home. It was more than they ever dreamed possible.

Six months ago, the bank took it back and it was sold to someone else after the foreclosure.

Terri cried for weeks after that. She tried to hide it from Ray, but he always knew.

But through it all, Terri never complained, she never blamed him, she never pointed fingers. She simply did all she could to be there for him.

She was his foundation. She was his life. But he *knew* Terri deserved so much more.

One month earlier, after she had walked back from her job as a waitress at Denny's to the trailer they were now renting, he sat her down on the dingy yellow sofa in the tiny living room of the only home they could now afford, and broke down.

He told her she *did* deserve a better life. That she *did* deserve better than him. That she *did* deserve someone who could provide for her.

He cried that he truly did not understand why she had not left him. That she was in her rights to do so and that he was now *begging* her to do so and save herself.

It was then, that his wife Terri—his rock, his foundation, his life— knelt before him and looked up at him with green eyes filling with tears. She then slowly placed the fingertips of her right hand under his chin, and lifted his face until he was looking at her.

"*Why* am I still with you? Because you are the best, most kind, and most decent man I have ever known. *Why* am I still with you? Because you are my soulmate, and I am so very much in love with you. *Why* am I still with you? Because when I married you Ray Thompson, I also swore an oath before and to God, '*For better or worse. In sickness or in health...*' I swore that to *God*, Ray Thompson. You *are* my life forever more."

Now, sitting in the cab of his truck sobbing, Ray was so very lost. In his mind, it was *his* mistakes that were now the cause of all her pain. *His* mistakes.

No matter what she said, he once again came to believe that she deserved so much more than him. And somehow, tonight, he was going to convince her of that.

He stepped out of the truck, wiped his eyes, and then entered their barely lit trailer.

And there, before him, in dim reflection of the one lamp they could afford in the living room, was the glowing and smiling face of an angel.

Ray Thompson could not remember the last time he had even seen his wife smile. Let alone, look so radiant.

Without saying a word, she took him by his right hand, walked him over to the end table with the lamp, and asked him to kneel next to her on the floor.

When he was next to her, she took out that week's copy of the four-page newspaper from their local church. She then folded it open to the third page and pointed at a small ad in the bottom right-hand corner.

"What is it?" asked Ray, as he looked from the page back up to her shockingly and amazingly happy face.

"It's a prayer answered, my love. It's a prayer answered."

CHAPTER TWENTY-EIGHT

Two weeks later, Christian was pacing back and forth in his office with Joan and Nina sitting in the two chairs in front of his desk trying not to get whiplash as they watched him try to cut a trench into his very expensive carpet.

"All ten of them are now in our conference room?"

"Yes, Christian," answered Nina. "All ten."

"How do they seem?"

"What do you mean?" asked Joan as she smiled over at Nina.

Christian kept pacing with his head down.

"Are they happy? Do they seem excited? Are they rested?"

"Yes, Christian," answered Joan. "All but one come from very humble backgrounds. They still can't get over the fact that you flew them all first-class and put them all up in mini-suites at the hotel in Dedham."

"That's the least I can do," said Christian as he suddenly sat back down at his desk and opened the manila folder holding a short bio on each of the ten compiled through both a phone interview as well as the screening process done by his own firm.

Christian had read each one several times already, but picked up all ten in his left hand and slowly looked at the names and the faces one more time.

Christina Marie—Dorchester, Massachusetts. Lost her daughter to street violence.

Winston McNeil—London, England. Recently lost his wife of fifty-two years.

Jose and Anita Gomez—Mexico City, Mexico. Married forty-six years. Empty nesters of deep faith looking for a calling.

Dimitri Kharlamov—Moscow, Russia. Forty-something. Incredibly decent. Desperately lonely to the point it is consuming him.

Carol MacKenzie and her sister, Dottie—Edmonton, Alberta, Canada. Carol, never married and 72, is in the early stages of Alzheimer's disease. Carol is the one who wanted to come and her sister Dottie, widowed and 78, decided she could not let her "baby-sister" go without her.

James Rawlings III—New York, New York. Sixty-four years of age and an incredibly successful former CEO. Worth north of $200 million. Christian had met him and his wife Jill at a few charity events. James is coming on his own; his wife filed for divorce when James told her of his plans. They quickly agreed to a $50 million settlement plus his wife kept the townhouse on Park Avenue.

Ray and Terri Thompson—Memphis, Tennessee. Ray is 33; Terri is 30. Ray was a decorated veteran down on his luck after a workplace accident left him unable to walk for months. Poor treatment by the VA. Couldn't find real work after conviction for forged prescription for pain killers. Lost home in foreclosure. Outstanding human being. His wife Terri never lost faith in him.

Christian closed the folder and looked over at the still smiling faces of Joan and Nina.

"What are you two smiling about?"

"It's real now, isn't it?" answered Joan. "It was one thing to see *SW1* in Italy but it's quite another to prepare to meet some of the actual Elves who will populate the ship. Men and women, who, after a series of confidential questions, answers and details *still* volunteered to be totally off the grid and dedicate a full year of their lives to helping children. Men and women who truly do personify decency, civility, and grace."

"Yes," Christian agreed. "It is so very real now. And they are very decent people. Maybe more decent than I deserve…"

"Christian…" stressed Nina with a mock angry face.

"Sorry. I know I promised you both not to beat myself up anymore—even though I still think I deserve another year or two of verbally acknowledging and criticizing what I had become…"

"Stop, it, Christian," implored Joan. "Let's just focus on the man you are *now* and the great good you are doing *now*. Those people down the hall are the living embodiment of who you are now and that's good."

"Thank you," smiled Christian. "Thank you both. I won't forget again. Now, going back to those people down the hall, I have been giving this a great deal of thought ever since I read their backgrounds. And it's a thought and I believe a *truth* that should have occurred to me before I even read their bios. It's a truth which should have dawned on me every time I looked in the mirror."

"And what's that?" asked Joan.

"That this project...that *SW1*...might be *saving* these people as well. It for sure saved me in every context of the word. At least for those ten people in the conference room, in one way or another, they have either been touched by the cruelty of real life, or are looking for a better or more fulfilling life. When my brother Paul thankfully got through to me and told me to '*become a Santa Claus all over again*,' my only thoughts in terms of a positive outcome were of the children we would be touching in one way or another.

"But now, after reading these bios, I am convinced that *SW1* will also be saving some good and decent people as well. People maybe like me who *are* lost in life, or who have endured the worst that life has to offer, and who do *need* to be part of something larger than themselves. Something that will give them a sense of belonging. A sense of kinship. And maybe even a sense of real family. That's what I think anyway, but given the still fragile and emotional state of my mind, I could be wrong."

Neither Joan nor Nina spoke for a few seconds as each was contemplating what Christian had just said and how that might apply to them as well.

"You are absolutely right, Christian," answered Joan with a bit of a faraway look in her eyes. "You are. *SW1* is going to touch so very many of the Elves—and all of us—in ways well beyond simply helping very deserving children. In many ways, being involved with *SW1* will be the greatest and most meaningful gift any of us have ever *received* in life. I know it is for me."

"Me as well," chimed in Nina. "For real. Now, is it okay to point out a couple of things about our guests in the conference room before we head in there?"

"Of course," answered Joan and Christian at the same time with the same quick smiles.

"Okay. Well, as you know, there is a couple in there from Mexico City. Very sweet but they don't speak a word of English. So…Maria Santiago—who is one of our top analysts but also originally from Colombia with Spanish her native language—is on standby to translate. Next is a man by the name of Dimitri, from Moscow. Luckily, as it turns out, he speaks fluent English. Other than that, all of them seem both super excited and super nervous."

"Yeah?" asked Christian as the smile already in place grew. "Well, not as excited or as nervous as I am."

***

After Joan and Nina left to give him a few minutes to focus before they would all walk into the conference room, Christian began to stare at the phone on his desk.

Mentioning his brother Paul and going over part of their very emotional conversation again caused Christian to think about his brother down in Texas, and how much he really meant to Christian.

More than that, he began to think again about how his older brother Paul was just as much a part of *SW1* as he was. While Christian knew he may have been the maestro bringing together and synchronizing the various instruments of the orchestra, it was his brother Paul who wrote the first draft of the sheet music.

Christian picked up his phone and quickly dialed eleven numbers.

His brother answered on the third ring.

"So, holy man," said Christian with a laugh. "Guess what we have on *SW1*?"

"You certainly sound more chipper."

"Yeah," Christian answered. "Maybe. When's the last time I spoke with you?"

"Not since you told me you were going through with this project."

"Whoops," said Christian in a genuinely contrite voice. "Sorry. I've been a bit crazed since then."

"Don't worry," laughed his brother. "I've gotten used to you ignoring me for long stretches at a time."

"Hey," said Christian after being stung by the reminder of his past behavior.

"My turn to say 'Sorry.' So…tell me what you have on *SW1*."

Since they were both boys, Christian had always felt better, more secure, and more at peace when talking to his older brother. A feeling that had only intensified once Paul had been ordained a minister.

"Oh, yeah," said Christian as he once again transformed into the excited younger brother. "We have a chapel. An honest to goodness *chapel*."

"Wow," answered Paul as his '*Christian is up to something*' radar was instantly activated. "I remember reading that some cruise ships do."

"Yeah, we've got one of those. You know what we *ain't* got, big brother?"

This was now more obvious to Paul than the giant Snoopy float going down 5th Avenue during the New York Thanksgiving Day Parade.

"Can I just hang up now, without you *ever* telling me?"

"We don't have a minister."

"Christian…"

"Paul…"

"I've got a church to run in Texas and a large congregation to shepherd."

"Too bad. That's why you've got an assistant minister. Give *that* guy a chance to save some souls and stop trying to hog all the glory for yourself for a change."

Paul burst out laughing over the phone.

"You're not going to give up, are you?"

"No. You're the one who pushed my 'On' button and started this whole thing. You're the one who brought mom and dad into it. *Mom and Dad*. So I'll just throw that right back at you. How do you think mom would feel if she knew—*and she will*—that her older son wimped-out and was only willing to talk the talk and *never* walk the walk."

"Really," said Paul who was now laughing more. "You're going to guilt-trip me by holding mom over my head."

"You did."

"But it's the North-*Frozen*-Pole."

"Suck it up, holy man. It's all part of God's creation. Or do you *only* minister when you are warm and comfy?"

Paul was now laughing so hard his eyes were watering.

"I'll have to talk with Karen."

"Yeah," said Christian now confident of the outcome. "You do that and then tell your wife that there is a nice little suite waiting for both of you on *SW1*. I'll send my Learjet to pick you up. Pack something *really, really* warm."

CHAPTER TWENTY-NINE

All ten guests—and soon to be Elves—were seated around the conference table. A few of them had inadvertently met in the hotel the night before, with the rest introduced to one another officially when Nina Sobhan had escorted them all into the room.

As they sat there is somewhat awkward silence, Winston McNeil spoke up.

"While we are waiting for Ms. Sobhan to walk back in with the chap who runs this operation, maybe we can introduce ourselves and say where we are from."

All nine other people nodded their heads or murmured in agreement.

"Right," continued Winston with a warm smile. "Brilliant. All right. So, my name is Winston McNeil, from London, England."

Winston then turned his head to look at the equally dapper man to his right with the thick white hair.

"Thank you, Winston. My name is James Rawlings, and I come from New York City."

"Christina Marie, from Boston, Massachusetts."

"Dimitri Kharlamov, from Moscow, Russia."

"Ray and Terri Thompson," said Ray. "From Memphis, Tennessee."

"Dottie Crosby and my sister Carol MacKenzie from Edmonton, Alberta, Canada."

Jose and Anita were next and were not quite sure what was going on. Just then, Maria Santiago, who had quietly entered the room thirty seconds earlier, leaned down between them and spoke softly in Spanish for a minute. As she did, they both broke out in smiles.

Maria then stood and looked at the group.

"And last, Jose and Anita Gomez, from Mexico City, Mexico."

The introductions broke the ice and everyone seemed to be talking. All that is, except Dimitri.

Over the course of the last couple of years, he had become more withdrawn and much more cautious when meeting people as a defensive mechanism to protect his mostly broken feelings and emotions.

"Hi, Dimitri. As I just said, I'm Christina, from Boston."

Dimitri looked up from staring at the highly polished conference table to see the smiling face of Christina Marie. More than that, she had her right hand extended toward him.

Dimitri looked at her smiling face and bright eyes, and then at her extended hand.

Pleasantly surprised and a bit shocked by the warm gesture, it took his mind a couple of seconds to register it all. When it did, he slowly brought up his right hand and shook hers.

As he did—for the first time in longer than he could remember—the smile which popped-up on his face was genuine and not forced.

"Dimitri," he answered as he shook the small but warm hand of Christina Marie.

"From Moscow."

"Yes."

"Your English is very good."

Dimitri swiveled slightly in the very expensive chair in which he was sitting so he could face her.

"Thank you," he answered while silently being astonished that the smile would now not leave his face. "I own a small café in Moscow. Over the years, a number of American diplomats and embassy workers would stop by for breakfast or lunch so…I slowly learned."

"Well…whatever you did, it really worked," answered Christina as she now swiveled her chair to better face him. "I wish I knew a second language. Many people from outside of Boston always kid us that we don't even really speak *English* here in Boston. Just *Bostonian*."

"Maybe they are just—how you say—*jealous*," said Dimitri as he raised his eyebrows. "I read once that England is the mother country for English. And that in all of the United States of America, there is only *one* city which comes close to the English spoken in London. That city is Boston."

Christina laughed.

"I like the way you think, Dimitri."

"So," continued Dimitri with a nod, as his mind was trying to recall how nice it was just to have a simple conversation and interaction with another human being. "As a Bostonian, are you a fan of your great hockey team?"

"You mean the Bruins?"

"Yes. Them. They have the face of a bear. No?"

"I think so," said Christina as she wrinkled her forehead. "I don't really follow the Bruins that much. I'm much more of a Pats fan."

"What is a...Pat?" Asked Dimitri

Christina broke out laughing. The first real laugh she had enjoyed in longer than she could also remember.

Just as she was about to answer, the conference door opened and in walked an incredibly stunning couple and Nina Sobhan.

The various conversations going on in the conference room quickly came to a stop as all eyes and heads turned toward the three people who had just entered the room.

As Christian walked in, the eyes of James Rawlings opened wide. After a second or two, he nodded his head as if solving a puzzle and then smiled to himself at his educated guess work.

"Ladies and gentlemen," began Nina as she stood at the front of the room slightly to the left of Christian and Joan. "I would like to introduce Christian Nicholas and Joan Randall..."

As Nina spoke, Maria Santiago knelt on one knee behind Jose and Anita and whispered the translation.

"As I mentioned to you all," continued Nina. "This man—Mr. Nicholas—is the one who created and is funding this project with Joan Randall as the one in charge of the, ah, *establishment* all of you will be living in for the next year."

Christian stepped closer to the table and looked down at the older, distinguished looking man to his left.

"Winston," said Christian as he smiled. "Thank you so much for being here. When things settle down, you will have to tell me all about your nephew Patrick and his political prospects. Quite exciting. Also, you will have to explain to me how you and Patrick became such devoted fans of Crystal Palace."

Winston was instantly touched and a bit surprised by the personal contact. Touched that this man clearly had done some research on him, and surprised, because he looked like someone created by Central Casting in Hollywood, and therefore didn't seem like the type of bloke who would care to do research on anyone.

"Well," began Winston as he quickly tried to organize his thoughts. "You caught me a bit off guard there, Mr. Nicholas…"

"Christian, please."

"Right, then. *Christian*. First, thank you for mentioning Patrick. Quite a young lad he is. Next, I am truly thrilled and excited to be here and really curious to learn more."

Christian smiled down at Winston.

"You are about to learn all there is to know and afterwards, I hope you will be as committed to the project as we are."

Christian next shifted his eyes to the well-dressed man next to Winston.

"James. It's so very good to see you again."

James Rawlings waited just a moment before responding. Much like a man very cautiously testing the thickness of the ice before putting his full weight upon it, Rawlings wanted to make sure his response would not cause catastrophic damage.

"Christian," smiled Rawlings. "It's actually great…and ironically *quite* comforting…to see you again as well. Ironic in the sense that we both find ourselves in the same 'un-matrimonial' state."

"Yes," answered Christian after his own cautious pause. "I was sorry to learn about you and Jill. But as for me…I am in a much better place now."

James Rawlings and everyone at the table quickly looked up at Joan and Christian who, for that split-second, only had eyes for each other. What everyone recognized—most especially Jose and Anita, and Ray and Terri—was hopefully, the beginnings of true love standing before them.

"I see," responded Rawlings as he nodded his head. "My instinct tells me that the lightbulb of what is truly important in life went off over both of our heads recently, which, in turn, illuminated some of the material and personal things we may have chased for years as nothing more than wasted white noise."

"Your instinct is one hundred percent correct, James," answered Christian with a knowing laugh. "In the next day or so, it will be wonderful to sit down with you and catch-up on a few things."

Christian next looked over at Christina.

"Christina. How nice it is to meet you for two of what will be many reasons. The first is you and I happen to share *only* the best name *ever*…"

For the second time in a long time, a real and natural laugh came out of her.

"…and second, you more than anyone else here, can explain to everyone why we—and I am a long-time naturalized Bostonian—have *the* best sports teams in the world."

Like those before her, Christina was instantly put at ease by Christian's charm, warmth, and the homework he had done.

"Well," she giggled. "I was just trying to educate Dimitri here on the New England Patriots when you walked into the room."

"Ah, Dimitri," said as he looked at the man from Moscow who was still smiling at Christina before looking up at Nicholas. "Thank you for being here."

"It is I who should thank you, Mr. Nich…*Christian*. The air travel, the hotel, everything," answered Dimitri.

Nicholas bowed slightly to Dimitri before looking back over at Christina.

"Christina. I should warn you that as you do try to educate Dimitri on the unquestioned superiority of our sports teams, you need to know that Dimitri's father played for the world-famous Moscow Dynamo hockey team, and that his uncle was simply one of the greatest hockey players the world has ever known."

"But how," began Dimitri as he looked over at Christina in wonder.

Christian then stepped further around the table before looking over at Ray and Terri.

"Ray, Terri," said Christian as he nodded down at the couple. "Thank you both for being here. Ray, I especially want to thank you for your service to our nation. Both my dad and mom were—like you—in the United States Army. Because of that, I want to say how very sorry I was to learn that the Veteran's Administration let you down, as they have so many vets, and that you should be incredibly proud of the man you have become given the multiple obstacles you've overcome."

Ray Thompson slowly pushed his chair back, stood, and then, when basically standing at attention, extended his right hand to Christian.

Without saying a word, Christian grasped it in his and then wrapped his left hand around it.

"Thank you, sir," said Thompson. "It's an honor to be here."

When Ray sat back down, Terri leaned over and hugged her husband tightly as tears of pride unashamedly rolled down her face.

Christian took another step to the side.

"Dottie and Carol. How wonderful to have you both here. We share a Canada connection. I have some cousins who live up in Sydney, Nova Scotia, and with regard to your hometown of Edmonton, the firm I run owns some shares in one of your large oil producing companies. I've had the pleasure of visiting Edmonton a few times. It's a great city with even better people."

Dottie and Carol shared a quick look as they smiled at each other.

"Thank you, young man," answered Dottie. "We both feel blessed to be here and a little shocked that we did such an impulsive thing. We simply told our family and friends that we were taking several excursions in a row and would report in from the road. I must say, my nephew did not like the mystery of it all and kept pushing us for details but we managed to put him off."

"Well, Dottie" answered Christian with a chuckle. "This is *the* most impulsive thing I've ever done in my life. That said, I've also never felt so certain that I am doing the right thing as I do now. As for communicating back home to those who love and care about you, we will make sure that is all taken care of in your name and that no one is worried. Ultimately…"

Christian then leaned down, put his right hand on the shoulder of Carol as he looked her in the eyes. "…there is nothing and *no one* more important to me and this project than all of you."

Christian then took one more step until he was in front of Anita and Jose with Maria Santiago hovering close behind.

"*Anita y Jose. Buenas tardes, mucho gusto, y muchas gracias por todo.*"

Jose and Anita instantly exchanged excited looks to know that the man in charge of everything spoke such perfect Spanish.

"Just so you know," continued Christian quickly as he looked at the couple and then up at Maria. "Me saying, '*Good afternoon, so nice to meet you and thank you for everything*' in Spanish is the absolute limit of my knowledge of your great language. That said, over the course of the next several months, it is my intention to learn as much as I can."

Maria knelt down behind them again and began to whisper the translation in Spanish. When she finished, Jose and Anita laughed in acknowledgment as Jose held up his hand.

"Th...thank you." Jose stammered just a bit. "And we...English."

CHAPTER THIRTY

Four days later, Christian, Joan, and Nina found themselves back in Christian's Learjet 70 as it cut its way through a deep blue sky at 32,000 feet on its way from the private airfield in Norwood, Massachusetts, to Norfolk, Virginia.

SW1 had docked at the naval base in Norfolk at 11 PM two nights earlier. Onboard were the officers and staff as well as Jeff Foster and his team.

There was only one thing missing: *The Elves*.

The screening process was complete. Aside from "The Ten"—as Christian had named the handpicked "Elves" he had just met—three hundred and ninety others—out of approximately fifteen thousand responses to the ad—had been selected.

As it turned out, the almost four hundred Elves joining the ten already selected were very much like them. Good and decent men and women looking not only to do something positive with their lives, but in many ways, to *have* a life.

As Christian discovered, the three hundred and ninety were simply a larger reflection of "The Ten." Good people who were either lost, lonely, confused, scared, wounded, looking for a mission, faith-filled, or a combination thereof.

As Christian looked out the window of the Learjet 70, the magnificence of the Chesapeake Bay came into view. While he could see it, he had no idea it was there.

His mind's eye was filled only by the four hundred men and women who would soon be living, working, and socializing in *SW1*.

As he thought of them, he was hit with a satisfying sense of pride.

When this unbelievable plan flashed into his mind the morning his brother reached him, his only goal was to bring a little joy and happiness into the lives of poor and disadvantaged children.

But now, because of a plan some for sure thought "crazy," *SW1* was doing so much more than that. So much more. It *was* reaching, touching, and "saving" the lives of a number of adults simply and truly worn down by the cruelties of life.

It was *not* an academic exercise. It was *not* a theory. It was not that word "someday," which really *was* code for *never*. It was a reality. It was a reality made possible because of Christian's pain. Because of *his* reality at the time.

SW1 was a reality now because *he* dared to dream it. Because he made it happen.

And now…and now…it was the most meaningful *bonus* Christian had ever received in his business career.

To give deserving children toys, food, medicine, and books was amazing. But to *unexpectedly* give grown men and women hope, renewed faith, companionship, a sense of purpose, peace of mind, and a sense of belonging was something else again.

It was a bonus like none Christian had ever imagined.

Out of the corner of her eye, Joan caught Christian slowly shaking his head. As she turned to look at him, she caught his reflection in the thick plexi-glass of the jet window. What she saw caused no confusion. No curiosity. For though his eyes seemed disengaged, his reflected smile said everything.

Joan was positive that Christian was thinking of the Elves. That his mind's eye had now taken him deep into *SW1* and he was "seeing" all the good he was doing and about to do.

For the first time since he was an eight-year-old-boy, Joan knew that Christian had *that* feeling again. For the first time in over four-decades, he once again *felt* what it was like to help human beings in need.

As he smiled out the window of the private jet with his mind inside *SW1*, Joan slowly reached over to hold his hand.

Not a word was exchanged, but everything was said.

***

Aboard the *SW1* were several meeting and conference rooms.

Christian, Joan, and Nina were seated around a table in one of the smaller rooms.

In front of Christian was a black, loose-leaf binder. Inside the binder were the backgrounds of all of the crew, staff, and contractors as well as every one of the four hundred Elves about to walk onboard *SW1* in eight hours under the cover of darkness.

Christian was having "The Ten" flown down from Massachusetts in his Gulfstream G650. As for the rest, each had business class tickets and were rendezvousing at the airport in Norfolk where they would be met by staff from Christian's firm and board private buses to be transported to *SW1*.

In addition to the Elves were eight individuals handpicked by Christian. Eight people who quite possibly had the most important of all skillsets. All eight were toymakers from some of the most well-known companies in the world. Three were from the United States, one was from France, two were from Canada, one was from Germany, and one was from Brazil.

As the project morphed from a vision, to a dream, to an idea, to blueprints, and to a reality, Christian was less and less surprised by the unusual or even impossible.

Amazingly, four of the toymakers had independently answered the ad.

For the four who had not, they possessed a strong desire to help children and be a part of something greater than themselves.

All eight understood the mission. All eight were there to teach the Elves to make the most basic of toys in the workshop. Toys for children in need that *would* be handcrafted at the North Pole.

Christian closed the binder and looked up at Joan and Nina with a smile.

"Before we start to talk about the 'miracle' needed to pull this all off, I wanted to point out something incredibly important."

"What is that, Christian?" asked Joan.

"Simple," said Christian as he jumped up from his chair in excitement. "*Look* where we are. *Look* where we are *right* this second. I mean, are you *kidding* me. This is amazing. We are conducting a meeting on *SW1*.

We are on it. On *SW1*. Something that didn't exist in my—or anyone else's mind a few months ago—is now a reality. Something that didn't exist even in theory a few months ago is now about to set sail for the North Pole. *The North Pole*."

Christian then began to—as Joan now knew was normal when he was either very excited or very nervous—pace back and forth while occasionally running his right hand through his thick black-and-gray hair.

As he did and most especially because of their developing feelings for each other, Joan thought he cut a most handsome figure in his blue golf shirt, his black khakis, and highly polished black shoes. The fact that he was six-feet, three-inches tall and weighed one-hundred-ninety-five pounds didn't hurt the image either, she thought to herself as he reached the far wall and turned back to face them.

"In about eight hours," continued Christian as he started the ten-foot walk back toward them. "Four hundred Elves are going to walk onboard and be escorted to the auditorium. Then, I am going to be standing before all of them welcoming them all aboard *SW1* and thanking them for their generosity and their belief in this project. *Simply amazing*."

Christian then sat back down and tapped the black binder.

"I've made a decision."

"Christian," laughed Nina. "You've made about a thousand decisions in the last few weeks."

"Yeah, that's true, isn't it? And have either one of you patted me on the back lately?"

"Well," answered Nina. "We would have but we didn't want to get hit by your own hand doing the same thing."

"Oh, jokes. My executive vice president has jokes. Fine. Then I've made yet *another* decision."

Nina pretended to be filing her fingernails in boredom as she tilted her head slightly waiting for the decision.

"When this meeting is over, Nina. I want you to cut *your own* salary in half."

"Well, gee," laughed Nina. "Since I've been secretly adding a zero to my paycheck for years and years, I guess that pay cut won't be so painful."

"Okay," answered Christian as he turned his head to look at Joan. "When this meeting is over, please find out where the brig is on this ship and have Marty and his team lock-up Nina for the next decade or so."

"Yes, Christian," smiled Joan as she looked at Nina and winked. "I'll take care of that right away. Now, in the meantime, why don't you tell us of your latest decision and then after that…go back to your suite and take a nice long nap."

"You think so?" asked Christian to Joan already knowing the truth.

"Yes, dear. You need a nap."

"Right," nodded Christian. "Okay, so before I go to lie down, I wanted to tell you both that I've decided to make Winston McNeil the supervisor of the elves."

"The Head Elf," emphasized Nina.

"Yes," agreed Christian with a smile. "The Head Elf. I like that."

"What a wonderful choice, Christian," added Joan. "Not only is he a very distinguished and decent man, but I read in his background that he was the manager of a Marks & Spencer department store in London for thirty-five years. He'll be fantastic for so many reasons."

"Thank you. There really is something very special about him. And to help him out, I'm going to make Ray Thompson and Christina Marie his assistants. Ray has real leadership skills he learned while serving our nation in the Army, and Christina has great people and management skills she learned as a supervisor in the Post Office. Like Winston, both have been through a great deal of personal pain lately and both are simply incredibly good people."

"They are," agreed Joan. "As are you. Now, to *keep* you special, get back to your suite and curl up with your teddy bear for two or three hours."

As Christian nodded and stood to leave, Nina opened the reminder section of her smartphone.

"Christian. Don't forget that *before* you greet all of the Elves we are back in here for a meeting with Jeff Foster to get the final update on all of the modifications made to *SW1* as well as with Mike Doble, who heads up U-FO-DRONE."

"Sounds great," said Christian as he sleepily walked out of the conference room.

CHAPTER THIRTY-ONE

Five hours later, Christian was back in the same conference room. Not only was he more refreshed from what turned out to be an extended catnap, but he had also changed his clothes.

In anticipation of meeting the Elves, Christian believed a black suit, a white French cuff dress shirt, and a blue tie would be a much more appropriate and respectful attire to greet four hundred people who were taking a leap of faith to leave their homes and lives to travel to, quite possibly, the most inhospitable and unusual location on earth.

Like Christian, both Joan and Nina had also changed; both were now wearing black outfits. Joan was in a black pants-suit with a white blouse, and Nina was wearing a black skirt hitting just below the knees, a matching jacket, and also a white blouse.

When the two walked into the room together, Christian burst out laughing.

"Well, it's good to see we all got the memo to wear black suits with white shirts."

Joan looked down at Christian and smiled.

"True, but you clearly were the only one to get the 'blue tie mandatory' memo."

Christian looked down and touched his Hermès tie before smiling back up at Joan and Nina.

"Well, rank does have its privileges."

With that, he stood and kissed each woman on the cheek before taking off his suit coat and placing it on the back of his chair.

Seated across from Christian at the conference table for six were Mike Doble and Jeff Foster. Both had known Christian for years, and both were mostly too tired to talk unless directly addressed.

Foster had come over with the ship from Italy. The week-long voyage had been anything but a vacation, with Foster devoting sixteen-hour days to make sure that everything was in place and in working order. Everything was except...the most important modification he and his team had made to the ship.

Mike Doble had taken the red-eye flight from San Jose, California, where U-FO-DRONE was headquartered.

Normally as the CEO of the company, he would not be taking a red-eye anywhere, but considering Christian Nicholas was the largest shareholder of his company and considering the shockingly unique assignment Christian had given him and his company, Doble felt it best to show up himself to give the progress report.

Like Jeff Foster's company, U-FO-DRONE now made most of its millions in profits from the United States government, originating from a contract that saw them deliver an assortment of top-secret drones to the Department of Defense, which were several generations ahead of anything the public could even dream about.

Tired as they were, both men rose to greet the two women who had entered the room.

"Okay, guys," said Christian after everyone had exchanged greetings and pleasantries and were once again seated. "Let's have it. Jeff, you first."

"Sure," answered the highly successful architect. "Not much to report. First, Marco's parents came over with me on the crossing from Italy. Not surprising, since their son is the CEO of the company that built this thing, they know more about the ship than I do. Next, my guys, in conjunction with the team still with us from Fincantieri, completed every retrofit needed to transform the ship into *SW1*. That said, we are still trying to work out some bugs in one system."

"Which is?" asked Christian as he raised his right eyebrow.

"The heating system we added to the hull of the ship."

"Oh," laughed Christian as he looked at his friend and business colleague. "You mean the heating system we *had* to have installed to ensure that when *SW1* is on station at the North Pole, the massive ice-flows on the Pole *won't* keep closing in on the ship and eventually crush it like a tin can. You mean *that* system?"

"Yup," answered Jeff with a smile. "That one."

"No worries, Jeff. We will be here in Norfolk for the next few days going through orientation. I have complete faith that you and the team will have it all figured out and working *perfectly* by the time we have to leave for the North Pole."

"That makes one of us," answered Foster with a grunt.

Christian turned his head to look at Doble.

"And what news you?"

Doble pushed his wire-rimmed glasses up the bridge of his nose and nodded his head.

"All great from my end."

"Teacher's pet," jumped in Foster with a laugh.

"Hey," countered Doble. "Can I help it if my guys are the best of the best and put the 'art' in state-of-the-art.' But don't worry, Jeff. We're always going to need buildings and people to weld stuff. You'll always find work."

"And the world is always going to need comedians," said Christian. "Which will be your next gig if the drones don't work as advertised."

"They do and they will," answered Doble. "We've actually been secretly testing ten of them for the last week way north of Yellowknife, in Canada. For our purposes, it was unseasonably frigid up there. Well below zero. Which was great. It meant we could carry out our tests in weather close to what we can expect in December. All ten drones carried five-hundred-pound payloads and easily stayed airborne for forty-eight straight hours. We've got this. They will all be onboard—with a handpicked team by me—next week and ready to go when needed."

"That's great news, Mike. Thank you. Really. Awesome news."

Christian then turned to look over at Randall.

"Joan. You wanted to give an update as well?"

"Yes," nodded Joan. "With regard to the ship, just a few quick things. First, when we leave here, she will be fully stocked. Based on the size of the crew and the number of Elves, our supplies will last a minimum of three years if needed. Additionally, because *SW1* will not be sailing the world, but rather, will be relatively stationary at the North Pole, we will have enough fuel to power the ship for up to five years without the need to refuel. Again…if needed."

"Well, that's okay," laughed Christian. "Hopefully, the U.S. government won't strand us up there when we will eventually need to bring *SW1* back for repairs and upgrades. If they do…"

Christian then stared at Jeff Foster.

"I have no doubt that Jeff and his team will invent a laser beam attached to the bow of the ship to simply *vaporize* the ice when needed."

"Yeah," laughed Foster. "*That's* going to happen. If I morph into that 'Q' guy from the James Bond flicks. If not, bring a bunch of matches."

CHAPTER THIRTY-TWO

Christian stood backstage and took a deep breath. Once he exhaled, he wiped his sweating palms on a small towel he was holding and placed it on a table off to the side.

He then looked at Joan and Nina and smiled.

As he walked out onto the stage of the twelve-hundred-seat auditorium of *SW1*, there was a tremendous buzz of a hundred or more conversations going all at once.

As soon as Christian stepped into sight, the conversations stopped instantly and all eyes turned to stare at him.

Off and on during his career, Christian had used the phrase "The silence was deafening." Now, for the first time in his life, he truly experienced it.

Once he reached the podium set up at the center of the stage, he stopped and reached into his right-hand suitcoat pocket and pulled out the small plastic Nativity scene he had had since he was an eight-year-old boy.

He placed the Nativity scene of the center of the podium, ran his right fingertip over the tiny smiling face of the Baby Jesus, and looked up.

Filling the large center section of the auditorium were four hundred men and women. White faces, black faces, and brown faces looking up at him. All very neat and clean-cut and all, very, very quiet. A few were quickly putting in ear pieces to hear a translation of what he was about to say.

In the center of the upper section of the auditorium were seated Jeff Foster, Mike Doble, the officers and staff of *SW1*, the contractors and specialists, and the toymakers who had also signed on for a year. Christian's eyes swept over them quickly before settling on the front row of the auditorium.

Once he did, he instantly broke into a huge grin. For there, in that row, were "The Ten." All smiling back up at him and all looking extremely happy, content, and...encouraging.

Their smiling faces relaxed him more than any pill or drink could ever have.

"Thank you all for being here," Christian began. "While I've had the pleasure to meet ten of you, in some ways, I *do* know all of you. Or...as much as one can learn from reading a short bio on a sheet of paper. You didn't make up any of that stuff, did you?"

Beyond "The Ten," a few smiles appeared.

"My name is Christian Nicholas and it's my fault all of you are here tonight..."

More smiles accompanied by a couple of polite laughs.

"All of you responded to a somewhat mysterious ad in faith-based outlets. Next, you went through a fairly invasive screening process, signed an ironclad nondisclosure agreement..."

Christian clapped his hands together like a vice and smiled out at the crowd.

More smiles, more laughs and some murmuring.

"Yeah. You don't *ever* want to meet the guy who enforces *that* thing. His name is Marty and right now he's chained in a dungeon at the bottom of the ship chewing on a great white shark he caught with his bare hands. That said, I *do* have the key..."

A small ripple of laughter, smiles everywhere, and a now relaxed buzzing.

"In all seriousness, I am deeply honored that all of you are here and more than a little humbled. Ultimately, you all answered the ad because you want to help children in need. For some, as I'm discovering, there were also other motivations. Wanting to be part of something larger than us all, being the other main reason...as it was for me.

"When I am finished with my remarks, a few—or more—of you may decide to go. And that will be okay. It will. You will be flown and transported home first-class with my deepest gratitude for getting this far.

"For those of you who agree to stay, please understand that it is indeed a one-year commitment. You were informed of all of this during the screening process. Just as you were told we would be spending the next year in a very inhospitable area of the world. After being told that, you all *still* agreed to come. Hence, why you are now all sitting before me. That said, I want to stress again, there will be no going home for that year and no personal communications with anyone at home. If you do choose to stay, we will always get messages to your loved ones letting them know you are fine..."

Now, loud murmuring and whispered crosstalk.

Christian tapped lightly on the microphone before him until the crosstalk stopped.

"*If*...you do decide to stay with us...you will be given a stipend for the year. Additionally, all of your rent, your mortgage, your utilities, and other incidentals will be paid by us. Everything."

Gasps, a few hands covering their own mouths, and shocked smiles.

"Also, as you may have noticed when you stepped on board, this is a fairly luxurious cruise ship. A cruise ship which will not only be your transportation to the undisclosed and very inhospitable destination mentioned to you all, but in fact, your home when we get there. After this meeting, for those who agree to stay, you will be escorted to your cabins where you will find your suitcases as well as a welcome aboard packet. The cabins you will occupy have been modified, improved, and enlarged with the balconies enclosed to extend your living space."

Christian then paused to extend both hands before him and then spread outward.

"Don't think of what you see now as a 'cruise ship.' For our purposes, it is not. In reality, what it soon will become is a little town. *Our* little town. *Your* little town. In addition to the work area on board, there is also a restaurant, a movie theater, coffee shops, several stores, a gym and spa, and a first-class medical center that will be better than most hospitals anywhere in this country or around the world."

More excited crosstalk, looks of happy astonishment, and smiles.

"Above and behind you is the highly professional staff, crew, and contractors who will not only be running this ship, but will be looking after all of us while we are here. That includes the captain, his officers, the engineers, maintenance staff, doctors, nurses, security team, and other specialists. Some of those specialists are expert toymakers. Some of those specialists—courtesy of the U.S. government—are experts on weather as well as experts on where we are going.

"So, that brings us to the question of your journey to date. Where *are* we going?"

Instant crosstalk, with those seated in front of Christian leaning forward or backward to whisper their thoughts, worries, or speculation.

Christian decided to let it die out on its own. After another thirty seconds or so, the auditorium again grew almost impossibly quiet.

"Okay. The reason all of you are here tonight is because *I* am here. So, let me give you the short version on why I am here. Over the last few decades, I became—*only* financially—one of the most successful people in the nation and even the world. But…the more successful I became… the more lost I was and the emptier I felt. While I finally hit rock bottom, life itself no longer made sense to me."

Scattered crosstalk, a few gasps, and even more than a few heads nodding in understanding interrupted Christian.

He took a quick sip of water, looked down at his Nativity scene, and then scanned the faces in front of him before continuing.

"When I could go no lower, or shame myself more than I had, my brother called to change and quite possibly…save…my life. He reminded me of the one time in my life that I was truly happy. That was when I was a little boy giving presents to children less fortunate than us on the Army base we lived on. My brother—who is a minister down in Texas—advised me to 'become a Santa Claus all over again.' So…that's what I decided to do for the rest of my life here on earth. I am becoming a Santa Claus with one goal in mind. To bring at least a flicker of joy and happiness to the poorest and most dysfunctional children on the planet.

"A very wise man once said the *only* true value in having a great deal of money, was giving you the luxury of not having to *worry* about money. I forgot that lesson for a very long time in my empty quest for materialism.

"Well, no more. I have my life back. I *know* my mission, and my destination awaits. My brother told me to become a Santa Claus all over again. And because I am a very literal person who really likes a challenge, my destination…*our* destination should you agree to stay… is…the North Pole.

"This ship, which we have named *SW1* for 'Santa's Workshop One,' will soon travel to and be stationed at the North Pole where we will make toys for disadvantaged children around the world."

More gasps, lots of movement, and increasing crosstalk.

Christian was not sure how to read all of that when something truly remarkable happened.

In the middle of all the crosstalk, commotion, and sea of excited faces, an elderly man in the center of the audience slowly stood. When he stood tall, he began to applaud. Next, a middle-aged woman behind him stood and applauded. Then a young couple seated toward the back of the auditorium stood and applauded. Then "The Ten" stood as one and began applauding.

Then the rest of the four hundred stood, applauded, and cheered.

Christian looked off to the side to see that Joan and Nina were hugging one another in happiness at the reaction from the Elves.

No one was going home. No one. All were going forward...*together.*

CHAPTER THIRTY-THREE

Too excited to sleep after the presentation, Ray and Terri Thompson and Christina and Dimitri agreed to meet outside of their cabins on Deck Eight after getting settled in.

Dimitri and Christina were right across the hall from each other with Ray and Terri being just four doors down.

When Christina exited her cabin, she saw Dimitri, Ray, and Terri just thirty feet down the hallway, talking.

"Oh, my goodness," said Christina when she walked up to them. "My cabin is so beautiful."

"I know," agreed Terri who reached over to give Christina a quick hug. "Ours is actually the most beautiful 'home' we have ever had. We have an enclosed bedroom as well as a small living room, a forty-inch flat-screen television, a dining room, a kitchenette, a gorgeous bathroom, and a ton of storage space. Just amazing."

"Yes," agreed Dimitri as he nodded his head. "It unbelievable what they've done with about three hundred and fifty square feet. It really is much more luxurious and serviceable than my flat in Moscow. Incredible."

"Great. Awesome. Our cabins really are wonderful," said Ray as he turned toward the staircase. "But can we go see the *rest* of *SW1* now?"

"Sorry," laughed Terri as she looked at Christina and Dimitri. "My big boy here is very excited about touring the ship..."

"*SW1*," said Ray with a smile.

"*SW1*," agreed Terri as she nudged her husband to calm down. "While I was exploring our cabin, Ray was studying the map they gave us of the sh…of…*SW1*."

"Yeah," said Ray as he now led them toward the staircase. "Terri and I once took a three-day cruise on Carnival Cruise line. The ship was great, but nothing like this. The modifications they have made to *SW1* so it can be on station at the North Pole are awesome. Aside from all of the balconies now being enclosed, they have also enclosed the open passenger decks. Meaning I can go out for my daily jog on the deck now. While it might be 40 degrees below zero outside, it will be a comfortable 72 degrees on the deck. Three laps equal one mile. Plus, they have a state-of-the-art gym and spa. Simply incredible."

"How nice for you, Ray," smiled Dimitri. "But…" he continued as he patted his round midsection, "I now need to give my empty stomach a workout. What do they have for that?"

Ray, Terri, and Christina all laughed.

"Actually," said Christina. "Now that Dimitri mentions it, I'm a bit hungry as well."

"Not to worry," smiled Ray as he pulled the map for *SW1* out of his back pocket. "There is a small café down on Deck Four which is open right now. It has sandwiches, soups, salads, soda, water, coffee, pastries, you name it."

"Really?" asked his wife.

"Yes. I'm serious. It's actually open from midnight until six AM, when the food court opens for breakfast."

"How do you know such things?" Asked Dimitri.

"Because I was reading the little orientation packet in our cabin as Terri was *ooing and aahing* about the designer soaps in our bathroom."

"We have *designer* soaps?" asked Christina with a laugh.

"I think we have 'designer' everything," answered Ray. "Mr. Nicholas is a multibillionaire. *Multi.* I remember reading about him in *Forbes* magazine. He is worth something over fifteen billion dollars. I think he wants us all as comfortable as possible as we all work together for this cause."

"I don't know about his past life," said Terri. "But I think he's a wonderful person. Ray and I talked about it the other night. When you look into his eyes, you see only kindness, compassion, and concern. It's really quite comforting."

"Yes," added Christina. "There is something about him that touches you on a deeper level. Empathy more than anything. When he speaks to you, you truly do believe that he understands where you have been and some of the pain you have endured."

"Well…that's right," agreed Ray. "He may be one of the richest people on the planet now, but he came from very humble means. He's one of us. He really is. The very fact that his wealth and then materialistic values messed up his own life for a few decades only added to his understanding of the lives of real people."

"This is great. Really," said Dimitri as they all stood on the landing of the staircase, "but can we all agree on how wonderful Mr. Nicholas and our cause is *while* we are eating a sandwich in this mysterious and magical café Ray mentioned?"

Everyone laughed as Ray led them down the staircase toward their midnight snack.

CHAPTER THIRTY-FOUR

Christian and Joan now sat a quiet table for two by one of the windows near the front of Sophia's in Westwood, Massachusetts.

It was past closing time, but the owners were more than happy to let them enjoy the table, the service, and the peace while the wait and bar staff went about getting the restaurant ready for the lunch crowd tomorrow.

Over dinner and dessert, Christian and Joan had been discussing how well the orientation for the Elves went and how everything was really falling into place.

Christian—who had given up all alcohol after his life-changing event—had a coffee before him while Joan had an almost full glass of red wine.

"Before we got off *SW1*, I had a really great conversation with Jim Rawlings," said Christian while adding one sugar and just a splash of cream to his coffee. "Really a very nice guy. Do you know what he said to me?"

"Not yet," answered Joan with a smile.

"That even though he just basically wrote his ex-wife a fifty-million-dollar check and gave her the twenty-million-dollar townhome on Park Avenue in New York City, he still wanted to help out with the expenses of *SW1* and donate five million dollars the first year. How unexpected and special is that?"

"*Very*, I will say to the man who is spending *hundreds of millions* of his own money just this year alone."

"Thank you," smiled Christian. "At least *now*, that's what I'm *supposed* to do with it. As for Jim, if you look at it apples to apples, proportionally, he may be donating as much as me."

"I didn't think of it that way, which makes it all the more remarkable and selfless."

"Yeah," said Christian as he shook his head in thought. "This project has filled me with so much happiness, wonder, and renewed faith. For years and years, I was around some of the most superficial, selfish, and cutthroat people in business and society. I truly forgot that most of the people in the world are not like that. I forgot that for well over ninety percent of the people on the planet, every single day is a struggle just to *survive*. I forgot that truly good people help each other and give of themselves expecting nothing in return. I also forgot that even among the super-wealthy and the highest of 'high society,' there are incredibly good and generous people who *do* believe that we are in fact our brothers and sisters keepers. Jim Rawlings is just such a person."

"Yes," answered Joan with a growing twinkle in her eye. "He is such a person and there *is* something very special about him. On that very subject, I wanted to tell you that while you were having that conversation with Jim on *SW1*, I was having a long conversation with Nina."

"*My* Nina?"

"The one and only."

"About what?"

"Life," answered Joan with a now more serious look. "Real life. *Her* life. She hasn't told you yet, but she's decided to come with us to the North Pole."

"No," answered Christian as he sat up straighter in his chair. "No, she hasn't. She said from the very beginning that she didn't want to go. That she would stay behind to manage everything from the corporate office here in town. What happened to *that*?"

"Life, Christian. Her life. *My* life in a sense."

"*Your* life?" stressed Christian in confusion.

"Yes," answered Joan before pausing to take a sip of her wine. "My life. Nina, like me, is in her late forties. Nina, like me, has dedicated a great deal of her life to her career…"

"But," Christian began to protest before Joan held up her right hand and smiled.

"Wait. Hear me out. This is *not* about you. You have been the best boss and best friend to her anyone could have. This is about the passage of time and real life. Trust me, I know what I'm talking about. She and I have a great deal in common. We even *look* very much alike give an inch or two. Dark eyes, dark hair. We both stay in shape by daily workouts. Add a few blonde highlights to my brunette hair and from behind, it would be hard to tell us apart. She was married a long time ago for only a few years because the guy was all about himself. But for the last twenty years, while we both *hoped* to meet someone, we devoted our lives to our careers. Oftentimes, as my sister Janice told me, to distract from the pain of loneliness. But, as my sister also recently told me, in the blink of an eye, five years becomes ten and ten becomes twenty."

"Okay," answered Christian slowly. "I get that and I agree with it. I've also thought about exactly that with regard to Nina. Maybe not as much as I should have prior to my personal little life-changing epiphany, but I did think about it. So why didn't she come and talk to me about all of this?

"Because she was afraid you might get upset and might say no."

"Oh, give me a break. She's like a little sister to me. She knows that."

"She does," nodded Joan. "But she also knows you are the boss. And she worried because due to the firm's needs here in Westwood, you would not let her change her mind."

"That's just silly. If she wants to come to the North Pole, she comes. As simple as that. I've got plenty of people here who can keep an eye on things for me. So why the North Pole? What changed? I do get the loneliness part of this. I do. Why not just quit the firm and concentrate on herself? One of the first times she and I talked about the project in private, she said the idea of being up there for a year scared her."

"What changed?" answered Joan with a knowing look. "Several things for her. First, *you* changed. And with that change came *your* infectious passion for this incredible project. Meeting the Elves changed her perspective. Like you, like me, and like everyone committed to this project, just being involved has made her exponentially happier. More at peace with life. She wants more of that. She wants to contribute. She now doesn't want to let it go."

"Wow," said Christian. "Those are real changes."

"Yes…" smiled Joan as her eyes lit up. "But there is one more."

Christian frowned as he narrowed his eyes.

"What's up with the cat-who-ate-the-canary look?"

"Well…" began Joan before reaching for her glass to take another sip of her wine. "Speaking of Jim Rawlings…"

"No way," answered Christian with a smile. "Jim Rawlings. She's *interested* in him?"

"At this point, she's very interested in the idea of being 'interested' in him. She has been very impressed by him, his manners, and his class. What you just told me only adds to that."

"He also seems to be a good-looking guy."

"That doesn't hurt," laughed Joan.

"Wow," answered Christian. "So, are you going to try to play matchmaker or something? Because that almost *never* works out."

"Oh, no," answered Joan with a definitive look in her eyes. "Not at all. I am all in favor of letting nature take its course."

"I see," said Christian with a smile. "Let nature take its course. I think Nina is very lucky to have you as a friend now, and I am even more lucky."

Joan reached over to hold his hand.

"Well," began Joan as she softly squeezed Christian's hand, "for the first time in my life, I'm feeling something very special and I'd love it if Nina got to experience that. I think she deserves it."

Christian reached over and wrapped his other strong and warm hand around hers.

"You *both* deserve it."

They both then sat at the table in a very comfortable, connected and content silence. After a minute or so, Joan spoke.

"I can't believe the Elves have already been on the ship now for a few days."

"Or that *we*—now *with* Nina—get on *SW1* tomorrow," said Christian with a laugh as he slowly shook his head in awe.

"I know," said Joan as she beamed across the small table at him. "Surreal."

"A surreal reality," laughed Christian.

"Thanks *only* to you."

"*Please,*" said Christian as he stroked the back of her hand. "Back at the peak of my hedge fund days, I used to tell my staff: 'We can spin the clients but let's never spin ourselves.' I quite honestly could not have done *any* of this without you. Period. While the literal idea was mine, meeting and getting to know you honestly gave me the will to follow through and get things done. All of a sudden, I didn't want to let *you* down. All of a sudden, I didn't want to disappoint *you*. Over these last few months you *have* become my rock and you *do* inspire me. You do. Joan Randall, the simple truth is that you make me a much better person."

With that, Christian slowly leaned across the table and softly kissed her.

"Wow," said Joan when he sat back.

"What?" asked Christian nervously as his mind tried to instantly decode that word.

"Wow," answered Joan with a smile. "First, what you just told me are the most meaningful and touching words I have ever heard in my life. Next, for a first kiss, that was really, really good."

"Really?" asked Christian as he did his raise one eyebrow thing.

"Oh, yes. As they say, you have to kiss a lot of frogs to meet your prince. While I have *not* kissed a lot, I have kissed a few"

"And, which am I?" asked Christian as an anticipating smile of happiness started to spread across his face.

Joan now leaned across the table and kissed him gently on the lips.

"Oh, Christian Nicholas," she began when she sat back. "What do they say in the legal profession? Never ask a question you don't already know the answer to. Let's put it this way, if *I* have anything to say about it, that's the *last* 'first kiss' I will ever experience...*Prince* Christian."

CHAPTER THIRTY-FIVE

At 2:00 a.m. the next night, the *SW1* was already well out to sea as she made a steady fourteen knots.

In front of her was an ice breaker on loan from the U.S. government.

"On loan," Christian laughed to himself with the knowledge that he was reimbursing the government for both the fuel and the time of the sailors on board. Additionally, the massive and highly reinforced ice breaker was carrying a few hundred thousand gallons of extra fuel. Fuel that would be pumped back into *SW1* once she was on station at the North Pole.

Christian and Joan were standing off to the side inside the bridge of the luxurious and specifically tailored Vista Class ship as they watched the captain and his officers do their jobs in expert fashion.

For Joan, being on a bridge was business as usual, but for Christian, not only was this a first-time experience, but it was all the more cool when he stopped to remember that he actually *owned* the ship.

"Christian," said Joan as she reached down and took his hand. "They are waiting for us down in the conference room. Including by the way… your brother Paul and his wife Karen who just barely made it on board."

"Well," smiled Christian. "Despite what he and some people might think, I *probably* wouldn't have left him behind. Especially since that's what he was hoping for in the first place."

Christian then pointed at the control panels of the bridge.

"Look at those screens and instruments. They are awesome. It's like being on the bridge of the Starship *Enterprise* or something."

"Yeah," Joan agreed. "It's really impressive. But to keep with the spirit of your *Star Trek* reference, if you don't accelerate yourself to warp factor eight, we are going to be met by some unhappy people we have already kept waiting," Joan looked down at her watch, "for fifteen minutes."

"Wow," smiled Christian as he turned to leave. "Sam Spade *and Star Trek*. You start quoting Captain Ron from the movie *Captain Ron*, then I'll *know* I'm in love."

"You mean as in, '*Always watch out for the ladder, boss*.'"

"That does it," laughed Christian as he stopped to fold her into his arms and hug her. "You're a keeper."

After a long hug, Joan stepped back and looked up into his eyes.

"I'd like that."

"Me, more than you," said Christian who leaned down to kiss her before taking her hand to lead her off the bridge.

***

Christian and Joan walked into the largest conference room on *SW1* to be greeted by Nina, his brother Paul, Paul's wife Karen, Jeff Foster, Mike Doble, Air Force Major Susan Winstead, the toymakers, and James Rawlings.

Christian immediately walked over to give first his sister-in-law a big hug before doing the same to his brother.

"Thanks for being here, Paul," Christian whispered into his brother's ear.

"Karen and I did have a serious talk after you and I hung up the other day. We both strongly agreed that my place is with you, here."

"You have no idea how much that means to me."

Christian then looked toward the end of the table where James Rawlings was seated.

He wanted Rawlings there because of his great business sense, his long-time management experience, and because Joan hinted *strongly* that since Nina was going to be there, maybe he could be as well.

"I thought you said you were going to let nature take its course," laughed Christian when she brought it up.

"I am," smiled Joan. "But even nature needs some direction and a push from time to time."

After Christian sat at the head of the conference room table and Joan to his right, he looked at the people before him.

"Sorry we're late," he smiled as he tilted his head toward Joan. "It's actually Joan's fault. Gee, you'd think she's never seen the bridge of a cruise ship before."

"Don't even try, Christian," laughed Nina. "Because no one is buying it. Not your brother. Not even the new people," she finished as she nodded her head toward the toymakers and the Air Force Major.

The eight toymakers and the Major all offered polite smiles knowing they were in the midst of friendly inside humor.

"Yeah," said Christian as he shrugged his shoulders. "Just a pathetic attempt to shirk responsibility."

"True," said Nina as she leaned over to pat the back of his hand. "But at least you get bonus points for bringing your keeper."

With the gauntlet now thrown before his feet, Christian couldn't help himself.

"Thank you for putting that out there, Nina," said Christian with now a mischievous, little-boy glint in his eyes. "And have you *met* James Rawlings, yet?"

At the exact same time, Nina blushed, Joan kicked him under the table and Christian giggled as he said, "Ouch."

"I *have* had the pleasure of meeting Nina," said Rawlings coming to the rescue. "And I look forward to continuing the conversation."

Joan and Nina both shot Christian a "hah, hah," look.

"I'm glad to hear that, Jim," said Christian now adopting a more serious tone. "And thanks for joining us not only at this meeting, but for already being so generous with your time and resources."

"My pleasure," said Rawlings. "And my thanks to you for letting me be a part of this truly touching project."

"You bet," answered Christian as he looked at Rawlings before taking in all of the faces in the room. "And my apologies to all of you for the late hour of this meeting. But as we left under the cover of darkness for reasons of secrecy and since we were all up anyway, I figured the sooner, the better.

"In that spirit, first, I'd like to welcome my brother Paul and his wife Karen. Paul is going to be the official chaplin for *SW1*. His first duty will be to start the, 'We need to avoid icebergs at all costs' prayer tonight and keep it going until we reach the North Pole.

"Next, I'd also like to thank Major Winstead for being here. The Major," continued Christian as he nodded toward the slim woman with short, salt-and-pepper hair and deeply tanned skin in the blue Air Force blazer and matching skirt, "is not only an expert on the North Pole and Antarctica, but is one of the best meteorologists in the Air Force. She and her team of three will not only be educating us on *everything* North Pole—and I should add that she has been most gracious enough to offer to give seminars to the Elves and staff in the auditorium—but will be conducting weather research for the U.S. government while we are on station at the North Pole.

"Next, I'd like to thank our toymakers gathered. You are the best of the best when it comes to building simple, old-fashioned, and durable toys. As all of you might need a day to get your sea legs under you, get acclimated to *SW1*, and to learn your way around *your* Toy Shop—which by the way, is on Deck One and is approximately thirty-thousand square feet—the orientation lecture you will give the Elves will take place at 10:00 AM on Monday. After that, the lessons in the Toy Shop should begin immediately and continue until every Elf is comfortable making the six different toys we have picked for this first Christmas season. I should add that after this Christmas, we will be bringing aboard four state-of-the-art 3D printers and will be able a make wide variety of toys specifically designed for the children of each country we pick. But for now…simplicity is the word."

Christian then turned to look at a somewhat portly man in his fifties with thinning blond hair whose family had been making high-quality toys in Berlin, Germany, for over one hundred years.

"Klaus. I've been told you have been elected spokesperson of the toymakers. So, I will ask you, how long do you anticipate the lessons will last before the Toy Shop can be working at maximum capacity?"

"On behalf of all of us, Mr. Nicholas," answered the man in heavily German-accented English. "We think two weeks more or less. Based on conversations I have had with Ms. Sobhan," said the German as he nodded toward Nina, "that will be about all the time we can afford as we are going to have to make between five to six hundred toys a day to meet the quota given to us."

"Yikes," whistled Christian. "That's a lot."

"With a dedicated team of four hundred and the relative simplicity of the toys selected," answered Klaus. "I am confident we can do it."

"That's great to hear. The captain told me that at our current speed, we should be covering about four hundred miles per day. Give or take dodging a bunch of icebergs once we get into the colder waters of the Arctic Ocean, we should be on site at the North Pole in ten days to two weeks. Basically, the same amount of time needed to finish training the Elves."

"*The North Pole*," Joan half said under her breath. "I still can't believe it."

"Yeah," said Christian as he first looked at her with a smile and then everyone else. "For me, it's like having the best dream ever...only I'm wide awake.

"And..." Christian slowly emphasized, "starting tomorrow, all of the public spaces of *SW1* are going to be decorated for Christmas. All of them. There will be classy sections with beautiful white-lit Christmas trees, elegant bows, flowing green garlands, and Nutcrackers for sophisticated people like Joan, Nina, and Jim. And then...*really, really*, cheesy colored lights, inflatable snowmen, Rudolph and Charlie Brown characters, and even a few Clark W. Griswold decorations for people like me..."

"Hey," interrupted Rawlings. "Count me among the cheesy people. I love that stuff."

Christian leaned over and high-fived Rawlings.

"Also," Christian continued as Joan gave him an amused look, "and at least *most* importantly for me, there will be a large nativity acene in the Lobby of *SW1*. A nativity acene which will honor the reason we all celebrate Christmas in the first place."

CHAPTER THIRTY-SIX

Five days later, Jose and Anita and Carol and Dottie and Winston stood side by side on the "Teddy-Bear" assembly line.

All five—along with *all* of the other Elves—were now dressed in their *SW1* standard "uniforms." The men could wear either red pants with long-sleeved green shirts or the opposite. The women could choose between red or green pantsuits or red skirts with matching red jackets or the same in green. All had to wear red or green multipocketed aprons with their first names embroidered in large letters on the front.

Santa-inspired hats were voluntarily, either red with white faux-fur trim or green with white faux-fur trim. Given the ship was now decorated for Christmas from bow to aft and everywhere in-between, and in the spirit of why they all had signed up, all of the Elves chose to wear the hats while in the Toy Shop with many wearing them during off-hours or during various seminars.

After a few days of lessons, it was now time for Jose, Anita, Dottie, Carol, Winston, and all the rest to test what they had learned in the "classroom" and turn it into an actual work product. In this case, twelve-inch-tall brown "teddy bears." Half would have a yellow bow on their head for the "girl" teddy bears and no bow for the "boys."

In addition to the teddy bears, Jose, Anita, Carol, Dottie, Winston, and the three hundred and ninety-five other Elves were also being taught how to make old-fashioned spinning tops, four-car (including the engine and caboose) wooden train sets, "Jack" and "Jill" in-the-boxes, a wind-up car, vibrantly colored wooden paddles with a red rubber ball attached by a twelve-inch elastic, and a wooden plane painted silver with propellers and wheels that moved.

Dottie, Carol, Jose, Anita, and Winston were part of the "stuffing" team. They were supposed to fill the teddy bears with the "perfect" amount of cotton ball material before it was turned back to the sewing team to seal the now finished teddy bear. The sewing team working with them consisted of Ray, Terri, Dimitri, Christina, and James.

Instead of making perfect teddy bears, the ten of them were producing nonstop belly-laughs as teddy bears were ending up with no stuffing in one leg or one arm, or ears were getting sewn to the face, or brown fluffy feet were getting sewn to brown fluffy paws.

Klaus was walking up and down the cavernous Toy Shop monitoring all four hundred Elves when he happened to stop next to their bin filled with their "Finished" teddy bears. He reached his right hand in and pulled one out. A teddy bear with no stuffing in its head and its left leg sewn to the right ear.

Klaus turned it around several times in his hands as his eyes grew wider and wider before looking at Winston.

"And vat do you call this?" asked Klaus with a crooked smile.

"Why, old chap," laughed Winston, "that particular model is called the 'We need more lessons' teddy bear."

"Yah," answered Klaus as he tossed the teddy bear back into the bin with a laugh. "You need more lessons for sure. And maybe I give you all some homework on top of that."

"*Homework*," said Christina with a mock shocked face. "Where is our union rep? I demand a hearing. This *has* to be a violation of our rights."

"*Nine*. No union on the North Pole," said Klaus as he smiled toward Christiana. "No rights. You are *Elves* now. You're supposed to make toys and smile and laugh all the time. That's all. I've seen the movies."

On cue, all ten laughed and smiled in true happiness as Klaus made his way to the next group of Elves.

CHAPTER THIRTY-SEVEN

Four days later, Christian was sitting in the dining room of his private suite onboard *SW1* having lunch with Joan, Paul, Karen, Nina, and James Rawlings.

His suite consisted of a large master bedroom with a private bathroom, a full-sized dining-room with a table for eight, a living room, a galley kitchen, and a guest bathroom.

On this particular day, Joan pretended that it was essential that James and Nina be invited to lunch to discuss logistics while Christian pretended that she wasn't matchmaking.

Instead of logistics, Christian sat back in wonder as James and Nina innocently monopolized the conversation talking about the things each of them absolutely "*loved*" about New York City which…as far as Christian could tell…was everything.

With each syllable exchanged between them, Joan looked more and more thrilled and even more satisfied with her *non*-matchmaking.

Just as James and Nina had moved on to confessing their shared love of the iconic Chrysler Building in New York, the phone in the living room rang.

Christian got up to answer it as Joan fractionally nodded her head toward Nina and James to silently say, "Are you *seeing* what is happening here?"

When Christian was behind Nina and James and just before picking up the phone, he looked over at Joan and pretended to give her a round of applause.

"Hello," Christian said into the phone after Joan had directed a smile of happiness back at him.

"Now?" Said Christian into the phone as his voice turned serious. "Yes, sir. I will be right up there."

After he hung up, all five faces at the table were looking at him in curiosity.

"That was the captain. He said that it's imperative that I come up to the bridge right away."

"Did he say why?" asked Joan who was familiar with every possible scenario that could take place on the bridge.

"Nope," answered Christian as he took his blue blazer off the back his chair and put it on. "Only that I needed to get up there. So…let's go."

"All of us?" asked Nina.

"All of you," laughed Christian. "Maybe you and Jim can talk about all the things you love about Madison Square Garden on the elevator ride up to the bridge."

***

After Christian, Joan, Nina, Paul, Karen, and James were buzzed into the secure bridge, they found the captain and first officer waiting for them along with Major Winstead.

All three seemed worked up about something thought Christian as he walked toward them.

"Thank you for coming up so quickly, Mr. Nicholas," said the captain as he extended his right hand.

Christian shook it as he looked around the bridge and then quickly at everyone on it.

"Sure," half smiled Christian, not sure what he was dealing with. "What's the problem?"

"Oh, no problem," said the Captain as he half turned toward the multiple reinforced front windows of the bridge. "I just thought you'd want to see it right away."

"See what?" asked Christian as he looked out the windows and narrowed his eyes in protection from the brightness of the snow and ice all around.

"*That*," smiled the captain as he pointed out the window.

Christian looked again and this time saw the naval ice breaker about four hundred yards in front of them. Aside from that, it was nothing but miles and miles of ice and snow.

"What?" asked Christian as he stared at ship. "The ice breaker?"

"No," Major Winstead answered as she stepped closer to Christian, Joan, Nina, Paul, Karen, and James. "*The North Pole*. We are here. *Exactly* at the North Pole."

Christian didn't say anything.

He couldn't.

He suddenly could not verbalize a word or a thought.

As if instantly in a trance, he slowly walked over to the front windows of the bridge and looked down at the ice and snow in shocked realization at what he had just been told.

The North Pole.

He was looking down at the North Pole.

He had done it.

They had done it.

The captain began to walk over to Christian when Joan reached out and grabbed him by the arm.

"Not right now, captain," Said Joan in a whisper. "He needs to be alone for a few minutes to process all of this in his mind. He needs some space. Maybe we can all walk over to the other side of the bridge and give him some privacy."

Paul immediately nodded his head in agreement.

"Of course," answered the captain in a whisper to match hers. "I totally understand. To see one's dream and vision realized must be overwhelming on a number of levels. He must be so proud. All of you must be so proud."

"We are," answered Joan as they all began to quietly walk to the other side. "We are so very proud...of him."

As Joan said that, she turned to see Christian place both palms of his hands against the cold glass and slowly lower his face until his nose was pressing against the window.

As she teared up in pride at the sight of the man she now loved looking through that glass at the emotional wonder of it all, she thought, "the little boy in him has carried us all to the North Pole. From the darkness of his own despair, he really has risen to lift us all."

CHAPTER THIRTY-EIGHT

After two minutes of pressing his face against the glass, Christian stood back, wiped his eyes, and then whispered to no one in particular, "Can I go out there?"

Joan broke away from the group standing in the starboard wing of the bridge and quickly walked over to him.

"Christian. Sweetheart. What did you say? Do you want to go outside?"

"Yes," he whispered still somewhat glassy-eyed. "Where is Paul?"

Joan turned and waved Paul over.

"Yes, Christian," said his older brother in concern when he was beside him. "Are you okay?"

"I will be," said Christian. "I will be if you go outside with me. Will you do that for me?"

Paul looked into his brother's eyes and without having to know the reason, saw that at this moment, there was nothing more important to him on earth.

"Of course, Christian. I will be happy to go out there with you. Why?"

"It's about Mom and Dad," answered Christian to his brother. "I want them to be on the top of the world with their two boys."

***

Twenty minutes later after being given the latest in sub-zero protective clothing by Major Winstead and her team, Christian and Paul stood one hundred feet to the starboard side of *SW1* on the frozen surface of the North Pole.

Respecting Christian's need for privacy while balancing the need to rescue he and Paul from the elements if needed, Major Winstead and two of her Air Force team members stood on the ice just outside the gangway of *SW1* as they kept a careful eye on Christian and Paul out on the ice pack.

Once he reached the spot he felt most comfortable, Christian reached into the canvas bag he was carrying and pulled out a large framed photograph of their mother and father, smiling in their Army dress uniforms. The photo was attached to a three-foot-long metal pole that was spiked at one end.

Christian pulled out a large rubber mallet. And then, in the minus-twenty-degree temperature, pounded on the top of the pole until the photograph was firmly secured into the ice.

Christian then placed the mallet back in the canvas bag and looked over at his brother.

"Will you kneel with me?"

Paul smiled and nodded his thick-hood-covered head as both men slowly knelt before the photograph of their parents.

"Hi, Mom and Dad," began Christian.

Paul looked at his brother and could see tears once again forming in his eyes. Tears that would have frozen almost instantly if he had not been wearing tinted protective ski goggles.

Seeing Christian's emotional state, Paul reached over and held his little brother's gloved hand in his.

"It's me and Paul, Mom and Dad. Can you see us? Can you? I just wanted to have a little family meeting," continued Christian. "We haven't had one of those since the two of you went to Heaven. I haven't talked to you as much as I should have these last number of years. Here, with just the four of us together again, I wanted to tell you how sorry I am for the bad things I did. I want to tell you how much I love you and how much I miss you."

Paul squeezed his brother's hand as his own eyes began to water.

"I want you to know," Christian went on. "That I'm trying to be your good boy again. That I'm trying to do something positive with the gifts and the blessings that I have. I am trying to recall and use all the good you taught me. I am. Look where we are mom and dad. We are at the North Pole. Can you believe it? *The North Pole*. I know I've let you down these last few decades and I'm very sorry. So very sorry. But... thanks to your other *very good* son here..."

Christian then squeezed his brother's hand.

"I was saved and I *did* find my mission for the rest of my life here on earth. I am going to try to help children in need. I am so very sorry for what I became and only want you both to be proud of me again."

With that, Christian leaned forward and gently kissed the faces of his mother and father.

"I love you, Mom. I love you, Dad."

Paul then leaned forward and did the same thing.

When done, both men stood, silently hugged, and then, with an arm over the other's shoulder, walked across the snow and ice of the North Pole back into *SW1*.

CHAPTER THIRTY-NINE

Carol and Dottie were having breakfast at a table for four in the six-hundred-seat restaurant on Deck Nine when Winston walked up to them with a steaming cup of tea.

"Might I join you ladies?" asked Winston as he bowed in front of them.

"Please, Winston," said Carol who had decided that after her sister Dottie, Winston was becoming her best friend on *SW1*.

Carol knew she was having memory issues and knew that Winston understood that. A couple of times over the last few weeks she had slipped and called him "Walter." He didn't even bat an eyelash as he continued on with whatever lovely discussion he had initiated.

Dottie also had grown to truly appreciate the always well-dressed and dignified man from the heart of London. Not only had he adopted *them*, in a manner of speaking, but they, *him*. They knew that he was a recent widower and Dottie, in particular, knew that each was helping the other either to heal or experience forgotten happiness and companionship.

To Dottie's way of thinking, *that* had become the "Miracle" that was *SW1*.

Everywhere she looked, friendships and true bonds of affection were forming among all the Elves.

The latest example for her was Jose and Anita had taken seventeen younger native Spanish-speaking Elves under their wings and now loved the fact that several came to see them as their surrogate parents while at the North Pole.

"Mr. Nicholas was right," Dottie thought throughout the weeks as she observed her fellow Elves both at work in the Toy Shop and after hours in the public spaces. "While the main motivation for all of us was to help children in need, for many, it was more than that. We needed to be made whole in one way or another, and *SW1* is doing that in so many personal and meaningful ways."

Winston sat down and picked up a spoon to push his slice of lemon deeper into his tea.

"I don't mind telling you two ladies," began Winston in a happy conspiratorial tone. "I feel a bit lonely up here on the very top of the world since that American ice breaker left us all by ourselves three weeks ago. It was comforting to know those blokes were right out there next to us. Now, if I understood Christian correctly, we won't see them—or anyone else—again until next July."

Carol took a bite of her scrambled eggs and then a quick sip of coffee before responding.

"Oh, Winston," she said with a smile. "You simply have to learn the trick of fooling your mind."

"And what might that be, Miss Carol?"

"*Never* look out any of the windows. I never do and for me, it's like living and walking around the most beautifully enclosed little town ever. I don't see the cold, the ice, or the snow outside. I *only* see the good that is inside. We don't need another ship or anyone else out there. All of us—I dare say the *citizens* of *SW1*—now have one another. We do. And right now, that's more than enough for me as I've never been around so many genuinely good, decent, and selfless people in my life...with present company at the very top of that list."

Dottie reached across the table to hold the hand of her little sister while Winston broke out in a huge smile.

"Quite right you are, Miss Carol," said Winston. "Quite right. That's simply a brilliant way to see and think of all of us onboard *SW1*. I shall adopt your 'thinking trick' immediately."

"I'm so happy to hear you say that, Winston," answered Carol as she first looked at her sister and then at Winston.

"Indeed, Miss Carol," agreed Winston. "Now…I was wondering if after our Elf work today, I might escort you two to the movies this evening?"

"What's playing?" asked Dottie, who now felt even more blessed to have such a kind, aware, and empathetic man such as Winston as their new and true friend.

"It's a double-feature, actually," answered Winston with real enthusiasm. "*Miracle on 34th Street* and *The Santa Clause 2*."

"The original *Miracle on 34th Street*?" asked Carol. "Or the remake?"

"The remake if that is okay with you. Both are wonderful movies but as one of my favorite British actors—Sir Richard Attenborough—plays Santa in this one, I'm rather partial to the remake."

"Well," smiled Carol. "In that case, we would be especially honored to go with you."

"Brilliant," answered Winston as the first feelings of inner peace he had experienced in a long, long time now flowed through him.

CHAPTER FORTY

Before Christian knew it, "D-Day" arrived at the North Pole.

"D" in this case standing for "Drone-Day."

It was time.

Just after midnight on Christmas Eve and just twenty-four hours until Christmas Day.

Tens of thousands of toys had been handmade by the Elves of *SW1* and were now ready. Those toys, along with nonperishable food, medicine, and children's books in numerous languages, had now been packed in insulated, weatherproof, shock-resistant red and green rubber containers that would be dropped to the ground by the drones. And for those drones flying to majority-Christian countries, pamphlets proclaiming and explaining the birth of the Baby Jesus had been inserted as well.

Knowing all of this, Christian was once again pacing back and forth.

Only this time he was pacing in the large conference room on *SW1* waiting for the U-FO-DRONE team, the Air Force meteorologists, Joan, Nina, Paul, and the others to show up for the final meeting before the drones took to the sky.

Because of the multiple countries and numerous time-zones involved, a precise schedule *had* to be followed.

Christian had been awake since 5:00 a.m. and didn't expect to get any sleep until late in the evening of Christmas Day.

To compensate for his anticipated lack of sleep, Christian had the staff bring one of the automatic coffee machines from the restaurant to the conference room earlier in the day. Before they did, he had them fill it with Peet's Sumatra coffee. His personal favorite.

He was now on his second cup as he walked back and forth from one end of the room to the other mentally reviewing all the steps which had to be taken to get the gift containers delivered on time.

As he reached the far end of the room, the door opened at the other end and everyone else began to file in.

Christian walked over and kissed Joan, while hugging Nina and Paul.

As the rest took their seats, Joan leaned into him.

"Are you all right, sweetheart?

"Yeah," smiled Christian. "If being nervous to the point of passing out is normal, then I'm just great."

"All will be perfect. I've been told that everything has been working like a finely tuned Swiss watch."

"That's what makes me so nervous," Christian laughed. "Maybe the spring in the watch has been wound too tight and is about to snap."

"I don't know about the watch, but *you're* wound a little too tight right now. Maybe dial back on the caffeine just a bit," said Joan with a smile as she looked down at the coffee cup in his hand.

"Never," he answered with a smile as he realized that everyone was now seated.

Christian and Joan took their seats and then Christian immediately turned his attention to Nina.

"So, Number One loyal assistant. What's the latest?"

"All is great, Christian. Truly," answered Nina as she moved her long dark hair away from her eyes to take another look at her smartphone. "Not only did our firm hire expert local consultants in each country to be on site at each group home or orphanage to report back to us regarding the arrival of the containers, but they will also stay on site to make sure that everything ends up in the hands of the children. Toward that end, we are also not only making a donation to each home *after* the packages arrive and the items delivered to the children, but are also making donations to the local politicians and governments to ensure the same thing. I just checked in with headquarters in Westwood, and was told that everyone is in place and all is ready."

"Amazing, Nina," said Christian. "Really, really exceptional work. Thank you."

Christian then shifted his eyes just a fraction.

"Mike?"

Mike Doble had planned to leave *SW1* before it set sail for the North Pole, but then came to believe that he was bearing witness to one of the most altruistic and wonderful projects of his lifetime. He soon felt a personal responsibility to make sure his company's drones worked as advertised and delivered every container as scheduled.

With that decision made, Mike had gone to Christian to ask not only if he could stay to see the deliveries through, but if his wife, Jan, could join him as well.

Christian was thrilled with the request and Jan joined *SW1* just before sailing.

"All is good, Christian," reported Doble. "Each drone has been programmed to fly to its specific destination and each container has been marked and scanned to fly with that particular drone. To be on the safe side, we actually have two bays ready to launch the drones. At the moment, we plan to launch them from the bay on ground, or rather, ice level, but also have the bay on Deck Twelve ready to go as well. Between the two decks, we have two large, high-speed freight elevators ready."

Just as Christian was about to call on Major Winstead, he and everyone else in the conference room began to hear a *rat, tat, tat, tat, tat*, against the hull of *SW1* as well as the hurricane-proof window of the conference room. The noise was sporadic at first, but then within seconds, began to mimic the sound of one jackhammer, then two, then ten, and then one-hundred.

"What in the world..." Christian said under his breath as he looked first at Joan and then the major before standing up and walking over to the window. Once there, he pulled back the heavy maroon curtain and looked outside.

What he saw caused his jaw to drop. It looked like a thousand sparks a second igniting on the window. With just the two seconds it took Christian to observe that, the sound against the hull multiplied to an almost deafening crescendo level.

"Major," asked Christian has he turned rapidly from the window.

By the time he did that, the Major was already on the phone in the conference room talking to one of her Air Force colleagues down on Deck one with the Drone team.

She covered the mouthpiece of the phone to answer Christian.

"Ice storm."

"A *what* storm?" asked Christian as the noise level in the conference room continued to rise to the point where Nina already had put her hands over her ears to protect them.

"Ice storm," yelled the Major. "They can literally come out of nowhere and are one of the most vicious, deadly, and unpredictable weather occurrences on the planet earth."

"You've got to be kidding me," yelled Christian as he rushed over to her. "Can this *ice storm* or whatever it is, stop the delivery of our packages tonight?"

"In their tracks," yelled the Major with a completely crestfallen and frightened face.

CHAPTER FORTY-ONE

"The spring of the Swiss watch just snapped," yelled Christian to Joan as he forced a smile on his face.

He then turned to look back at the major.

"What *now*?"

She covered the mouthpiece again. "Bay One is out of the question at the moment. One of my guys just stepped out to look and literally almost had his face shredded. These things can materialize out of nowhere and last for hours or even—I'm afraid—days. I need to get up to the bay on Deck Twelve right away."

"What difference will that make?" Asked Christian as Joan came over to stand by his side.

The major hung up the phone and turned to face Christian.

"An ice storm at the North Pole really is a very strange phenomenon. It literally becomes a river of millions upon millions of flying ice particles accelerating through the air at over one hundred miles per hour. Razor sharp ice chips which, if you hold a thick cardboard box outside, will rip through one end and come out the other without slowing one bit. No human and no drone would survive inside of one."

"Then why do you need to get up to Deck Twelve?" yelled Christian. "How does that help?"

"Because," answered the major, who now stood between Christian and Joan in an effort to make herself heard. "These things are weird. As vicious and as wide across as they are—which can be miles—many times, they only rise ten, twenty, or forty feet above the surface of the snow and ice. I need to get to the bay on Deck Twelve to see for myself."

"I'm coming with you," Christian screamed.

"Not without a parka, helmet, goggles, and face protection. Neither one of us will last a minute if it does hit us while we are trying to stick our heads out there."

***

When they got to the bay on Deck Twelve, they found the major's Air Force colleagues already there along with the team from U-FO-DRONE. Like Christian and the major, all were dressed from head to toe in what passed for a modern-day sub-zero suit of armor.

Not one inch of skin was exposed, and not one person was recognizable.

And not one person needed such protection.

When Christian inched his way closer and closer to the open bay, he was met with the most surreal and unimaginable sight of his life.

Just five feet below the open bay of Deck Twelve, which was over ninety feet above the "ground" level of the ice and snow of the North Pole, raged something from an alien world condemned to a frozen eternity.

For as far as the eye could see, ice needles and splinters glittered like diamonds as they raced around and collided with *SW1* while reflecting the light of the full moon in the cloudless star-filled sky above.

"Amazing," screamed Christian as he looked down at an endless moving slab of incandescent, violent ice. It was as flat as the deck he was standing on and only five feet below him.

Mike Doble quickly slid to a stop next to him.

"My guys can launch from here. We can still launch the drones. We can keep on schedule," he screamed as he pounded Christian on his parka-covered back.

Christian shook his head.

What Doble was screaming at him had still not sunk into his mind as he watched the horizontal field of white razorblades slam into *SW1* at over one hundred miles per hour just feet below him.

Doble then grabbed Christian by the shoulders and turned him around to face him.

"Christian," he yelled as the saliva in his mouth began to freeze from standing inside the open bay, which was exposed to the now forty-five below zero temperature outside. "It's okay. We can launch. We can launch."

This time, it did sink in.

"We can launch," Christian mumbled to himself. "We can launch."

Christian's next thought was that this was a miracle. If this freak-Hellish ice storm had been just a few feet higher, all would have been lost. Just a few feet higher and everything he, the Elves, and everyone had worked and struggled for these last few months, would have been for nothing.

And yet...for a few feet...they could still launch.

The drones would fly. The containers would be delivered. And tens of thousands of needy, deserving, and abandoned children would get a toy, a book, some food, and some medicine.

They could launch.

***

For the next few hours, Christian ironically and quite appropriately stayed almost frozen in place on the open bay on Deck Twelve watching the U-FO-DRONE and Air Force teams successfully launch wave after wave after wave of preprogrammed drones into the star-filled sky of the North Pole. Each "Super-Drone," as Christian had come to call them because of their advanced and still top-secret technology, carrying a predetermined container to a specific orphanage or group home for abandoned children.

With those critically important missions now miraculously launched, there was one more Christian needed to carry out. For that, he needed to get back to his suite to shower, change, and pick up a package of his own that had been specially delivered to him by his brother Paul.

CHAPTER FORTY-TWO

Christian stood by himself in the beautifully decorated four-level grand lobby of *SW1*. Everywhere he looked were Christmas lights, green garland, and red bows.

On one side of the floor of the grand lobby stood a sixteen-foot-high Christmas tree with brightly colored wrapped presents beneath it.

On the other side of the lobby was a six-foot-tall, eight-foot-wide Nativity scene.

It was in front of the Nativity scene that Christian stood...alone.

Prior to his coming down, Nina had been nice enough to make sure that Christian would have total privacy in the lobby. He needed time not only to reflect, but to prepare.

Wearing a black suit, white shirt, and red Christmas tie with Santa cufflinks, Christian turned to face the Nativity scene.

As he did, his eyes shifted from Joseph, to Mary, to the Baby Jesus, to the manger, to the animals, and then to each all over again.

The overhead lights of the lobby had been turned off so that the only illumination was coming from the surrounding Christmas lights as well the soft yellow lighting within the Nativity scene.

Christian knelt in front of the Nativity scene and smiled at the faces that were smiling back at him.

"I'm a little rusty with these," he smiled at Joseph, Mary, and the Baby Jesus. "But a prayer of thanks from me would be *really* appropriate right about now."

Christian then bowed his head and silently prayed.

Just as he finished, he heard one of the three glass-encased elevators of the grand lobby start to move.

He stood to see the center elevator moving downward from Deck Four toward the lobby. As it passed Deck Three, he saw Joan standing alone inside. Just as he saw her, she saw him and both broke into spontaneous smiles.

Christian quickly walked around the bank of the elevators to greet her when the doors opened.

The sight of her stepping out of the elevator took his breath away. She was dressed in a candy apple red skirt with a matching red jacket, a white blouse, and red pumps. Her beautiful black hair was down and her dark eyes seemed to radiate a light of their own as she reached her hands out to Christian.

He leaned down, gave her a soft kiss on the lips, and then folded her into his arms and held her tight for several seconds.

When he stepped back, she looked up into his handsome face. A face that truly seemed to be at peace.

"Is everything, all right, sweetheart?" Asked Joan. "Nina said you wanted me to meet you down here before we go to the auditorium."

Christian nodded his head. Without saying a word, he took her left hand in his right and led her to the center of the lobby directly between the Nativity scene and the Christmas tree.

Once there, he stole a quick look at his watch to confirm the timing he sought. It was now just after midnight on Christmas Day. He next reached into his right suitcoat pocket and took out a small blue box.

He knelt on one knee to look up at the most beautiful woman and the best person he had ever known.

Joan brought up her right hand to her mouth.

"Christian..." she whispered as her eyes began to water.

Christian opened the small blue box.

He then took out a simple white gold ring with a very small diamond in the center.

"This was my mom's wedding ring," said Christian as a tear made a track down the right side of his face. "Joan. Will you marry me?"

Joan knelt down next to him and held his face in her hands.

"Yes, Christian. I will marry you."

They each then leaned forward and kissed.

Christian then stood and effortlessly lifted her back onto her feet as he hugged her again.

"I never thought this day would ever come," whispered Joan. "And now, I can't imagine ever being without you."

"This has become a time and a day of dreams realized," said Christian as he held her. "You are *my* dream, Joan. You are. Paul managed to save me so you could complete me."

They kissed again.

Christian then stood back and looked down at his watch.

"Speaking of dreams realized, we have an auditorium of Elves waiting for us."

Hand in hand, they walked toward the auditorium of *SW1*.

***

As the last of the four hundred Elves filed into the twelve-hundred-seat auditorium at *SW1*, Christian Nicholas paced back and forth on the stage.

Once all had settled in, he stopped pacing not only to look at them, but to burn the image into his mind's eye and memory forever. These were the first. These were the incredibly special people who took an amazing leap of faith not only to join him in this quest, but to make it a reality.

In one way or another, he truly considered all four hundred to be friends. For they now shared a very sacred bond that could never be broken. But of the four hundred, ten had touched him so very deeply.

Even though he was a changed man and his mission and time at *SW1* had only made him better by the day, Christian still had ongoing doubts as to whether—because of his previous wasted hedonistic lifestyle—he was even worthy of the blessings of God or the friendship of such decent and giving people.

Worthy or not, he was determined to continue to do all in his power to earn those blessings and the friendship and respect of those at *SW1*.

As the final Elf took her seat, Christian rubbed his hands together and slowly walked up to the podium.

As he did, Joan and Paul stood off to the side of the stage. Joan quickly and proudly showed Paul her new engagement ring. A ring he had brought with him to *SW1* from Texas.

Christian looked down at a white sheet of paper in his right hand and then back up at the curious and excited faces of the four hundred plus people seated before him.

He cleared his throat a couple of times, and then he began to speak.

"Merry Christmas, everyone. Merry Christmas. Despite the brutal and unprecedented ice storm all of us very unexpectedly just experienced, I am thrilled to say that all five hundred drones were launched. All five hundred. We just delivered approximately one hundred thousand handmade toys—toys made by all of you—to thousands of deserving children around the world. Along with those toys, we delivered food, books, medicine, and to those nations which *do* celebrate Christmas, thousands of pamphlets proclaiming the birth of the Baby Jesus and why He was sent down from Heaven. For that, I say congratulations, thank you, and a very Merry Christmas again to you all."

The four hundred men and women gathered before him erupted into cheers, applause, hugs, and tears of joy.

Christian gave them a minute or two to celebrate before gently tapping the microphone attached to the podium until the auditorium became mostly quiet again as now four hundred beaming and proud faces turned to look up at him on stage.

Christian hesitated again as he tried to look at every person in the eye before speaking.

"With that incredible news now delivered…I am going to ask all of you the two questions that make me very nervous. First, by a show of hands, with our first *Operation Bethlehem* now a complete success, who among you would like to *leave SW1* and go back home to your regular lives?"

Christian steeled himself as he scanned the audience. As he looked from side to side, he heard an increased murmuring from the Elves, saw lots of movement as the Elves whispered to one another, but not one hand went up. Not one.

He then turned to look back at Joan and his brother Paul, both of whom were giving him a thumbs-up.

Christian then turned around to face his audience of newfound and precious friends.

"Okay, then," smiled Christian. "Next and last question. Ready? Who would like to *stay* for one more year to try and top what we just accomplished?"

Almost before he got the words out of his mouth, four hundred hands shot straight up into the air with the loudest roar of approval Christian had ever heard in his life.

As the roar subsided and the hands went down, one hand, the right hand of Winston McNeil remained raised.

As Winston was one of the first "Ten," Christian not only knew him well, but had a very special place in his heart for this true gentleman whom he had named the "Head-Elf."

"Yes, Winston," said Christian as he looked down at the smiling face of the older man.

"Christian," answered Winston as he stood to look around at everyone in the auditorium before turning back to face Nicholas. "I know I speak for everyone here when I say…when I tell you that…that…we *are* home. We are home. Thanks to you, Christian, for the first time in a very long time, we are *all* home now. This…*SW1*…is our home for as long as you will have us."

Once again, the auditorium burst into joyful noise as the Elves jumped to their feet to applaud and yell their confirmation of what Winston had just stressed to Christian.

"Thank you, Winston," said Christian when the roar of approval subsided. "Thank you for saying that. This is my home as well. Now…" he continued as he turned his head quickly to look at his brother, "for those of you who would like to stay, my brother the chaplain will be holding midnight services here in just a bit."

With that, he slowly walked back to stand next to Joan and Paul. As soon as he did, all three embraced in a silent hug for several seconds.

When they separated, Minister Paul looked at his younger brother in admiration and pure love.

"First, congratulations on your engagement, little brother. You are both blessed. Next," continued Paul as he waved his right hand toward the Elves, "congratulations on all of this. You did it. You really did."

"No," said Christian as he stood between Paul and Joan. "We did it. We did it. All of us."

Christian then turned to face his older brother.

"And let's not forget that thanks *only* to you…and your boss," smiled Christian as he looked toward the ceiling, "that I am even here. That I was given a second chance in life. A chance to do something useful with my life, with my blessings, and with my gifts. So…thank *you*, big brother. I love you."

"I love you too, Christian. More than ever."

The minister then looked over at Joan and then back at his little brother.

"Now," he said. "If you two don't mind, I'm going to take my place with the rest of the Elves and give you a little privacy."

As Paul stepped off the stage, Joan stepped closer to Christian.

"I am so very proud of you, Christian. So very proud. This is the most amazing and surreal moment of my life. I am standing in a secret facility hidden in and around the snow and ice of the North Pole still not quite believing that we…that you…just basically magically delivered toys to thousands of little boys and girls and saved a number of adults here in the process…me included. I am simply stunned by the goodness of it all."

Christian reached out for Joan's hands.

"Thank you. But…to tell you the truth…you haven't seen anything yet. Wait until you see what I have in mind for *next* Christmas."

Joan shook her head as she laughed in joy. "I can only imagine."

"No," smiled Christian as he folded the love of his life into his arms. "No…actually…you can't. You can't imagine it because I *know* what it is and even I can't believe I'm going to try it."

Joan closed her eyes as she pressed her head against Christian's strong chest. She had never felt so happy, so safe, or so needed in her entire life.

"Merry Christmas, my soon-to-be husband," she whispered.

Christian leaned down and softly kissed the top of her head before looking over it to watch the four hundred plus Elves of *SW1* continue to hug one another, high-five one another, and pat one another on the backs because of their labor of love, which was at that exact moment touching children in need around the world.

Christian closed his own eyes as he rested his chin on the top of Joan's head in thought. In a world filled with too much pain, too much suffering, and too much sadness, they had just made an actual difference. While miniscule in proportion, what they just accomplished was done in love, because of faith, and in the *true spirit* of Christmas.

Christian then hugged Joan tightly.

"Thank you, my Joan. It's the Merriest and most meaningful Christmas of my life. It's what…I was meant to do."

THE END

ABOUT THE AUTHOR

D. Michael MacKinnon is a bestselling author who had the honor to write for two presidents while serving in The White House and was a senior official at the Pentagon.

Please feel free to reach out to the author at: dmacnorthpole@gmail.com